USBORNE ILLUSTRATED HANS CHRISTIAN ANDERSEN'S FAIRY TALES

USBORNE ILLUSTRATED Hans Christian Andersen's Fairy Tales

Retold by Anna Milbourne,
Gillian Doherty & Ruth Brocklehurst

Illustrated by Fran Parreño

CONTENTS

The Princess and the Pea 7

The Emperor's New Clothes 21

Thumbelina 41

The Ugly Duckling 67

The Little Mermaid 85

The Emperor and the Nightingale 111

The Flying Trunk 125

The Brave Tin Soldier 147

The Wild Swans   163

The Little Fir Tree   189

The Tinderbox   209

The Snow Queen   235

About Hans Christian Andersen   273

THE
PRINCESS
AND THE PEA

Once, long ago, there was a prince
who wanted a wife. "She has to be
a real princess," he told his mother.
"Naturally," the queen agreed.
And so the prince set off on his
horse to find himself a bride.

First, he visited a nearby kingdom whose princess was famous for her beauty. Indeed, she was breathtakingly lovely. However, she had nothing to say for herself, and every time the prince tried to talk to her about something, she yawned and said, "I'm bored."

The following day, he went to visit another kingdom. There he met a princess who had plenty to say about everything; so much, in fact, that the prince couldn't get a word in edgeways.

He continued his search. Further and further he went. He met princesses who liked riding horses and princesses who liked playing harps, princesses who were astonishingly clever or had perfect singing voices. But, try as he might, he couldn't find the one for him.

Eventually he returned home. "I didn't find

my real princess," he told his parents sadly.
"I don't think I will ever find her."

"But you must have met hundreds of
princesses," said his father.

"Thousands," the prince agreed gloomily.

"And not one suited you?" his mother asked.

"None of them seemed quite like a *real*
princess," said the prince.

"They were all daughters of real kings
and queens?" the king asked.

The prince nodded.

The king rubbed his
beard. "How much more
real can a princess be?"
he puzzled.

The prince shrugged,
and they left it at that.

Then one evening, as a terrible storm raged outside, somebody came knocking at the palace gate. The old king himself went to open it.

Outside stood a girl about the same age as his son, looking extremely bedraggled. She was drenched from head to toe. Her hair hung in rats' tails around her shoulders and her dress was splattered with mud.

"Good evening," she said. "I heard the prince of this kingdom is searching for a bride. I would like to meet him, please."

"I'm sorry," said the king. "He's looking for princesses only, I'm afraid."

"I *am* a princess," the girl answered.
"I'm sorry to have arrived in such a mess.
I was caught in the rain..."

"I do apologize," said the king. He invited
the girl inside, and sat her by the fire to get
warm. Then he went to find his wife and son.

The prince's face brightened considerably
as soon as he saw the princess, but the queen
frowned at the soggy girl and asked, "Whatever
brings you here in the pouring rain?"

The princess explained that she had come
from very far away, and that her carriage had
stopped in the next city for the night. "The
horses and all the footmen were too tired to go
on. But I couldn't wait to meet you all, and so I
decided to walk," she explained. "Unfortunately
a storm struck up while I was on my way."

The prince smiled warmly at that, but the queen looked rather doubtful. "I suppose there's no question of you going back to the town this evening," she said. "We will have a room made up for you and you can stay the night."

"That's very kind," said the princess.

The queen went herself to supervize the preparation of the room. Her son followed her out, whispering, "I think she might be the one. You can just tell she's a real princess, can't you?"

"She could be anybody," his mother replied. "But I think in the morning things will be clearer..." She left her son with their visitor and beckoned the maids to follow her upstairs.

She told them to bring twenty mattresses and pile them all on top of one another. Then she asked for twenty soft blankets

and twenty silken sheets to be piled on top of
the mattresses. By the time they had finished,
the princess's bed almost reached the ceiling.

"Now," said the queen. "I want you to bring
me a single dried pea from the kitchen."

"A pea, your highness?" the maid asked,
uncertain whether she could have heard correctly.

"A pea," the queen repeated.

When the pea was brought to her, the queen pushed it beneath the bottom mattress.

Then she went back downstairs, where the princess and her son were talking intently by the fire.

"Where was it you came from?" the queen asked, and the princess told them all about her distant homeland. She spoke with great fondness of the people who lived there.

"You have come a very long way to find a husband," said the queen. "Didn't you have any suitors nearer home?"

"I did," said the princess. "The young men I met were all very lovely, in their own ways. But none of them was the right prince for me."

"I know just what you mean," the prince agreed, beaming from ear to ear.

The prince and princess chatted away merrily all evening, until finally the queen said, "It's getting late. It's time we all went to bed."

So they said goodnight, and the queen showed the girl to the bedroom she'd prepared. When the princess saw the tall bed that awaited her, she was very surprised. "It looks wonderfully comfortable," she said politely. "But how ever will I climb into it?"

"With a ladder," said the queen. She nodded to a pair of footmen, who rushed away and came back with a long ladder. They set it against the bed and stood to either side.

"Good night, Your Majesty. Thank you again," said the princess, and she climbed up the ladder to bed.

"Good night," said the queen.

In the morning, the queen went to wake the princess. She drew back the curtains, peered up at the towering mattresses and called, "Good morning. Did you sleep well?"

When the princess's face appeared, looking pale and not at all well rested, the queen looked strangely pleased. "Come down to breakfast, and we'll talk there," she said, and bustled off.

The princess was the last to arrive at breakfast. She had washed her face, and combed her hair, but still looked very sleepy.

"Would you like to come for a horse ride with me this morning?" the prince asked.

"I'd love to," the princess replied, but she couldn't help but stifle a yawn.

"You seem very tired," said the queen. "Now tell me, how did you sleep?"

The princess looked embarrassed. "I don't want to be rude," she said reluctantly, "because you've been so very generous…"

"Go on," urged the queen.

"I slept terribly," the princess confessed. "Despite all those soft mattresses, I tossed and turned the whole night long. There seemed to be something small and hard right in the middle of my bed."

Everyone was surprised when the queen's face lit up. "How splendid," she said. She rang a bell, and a maid hurried in with a velvet cushion in her arms. On top of the cushion was a single pea.

"This was the source of your discomfort," said the queen. "And now I know beyond all doubt that you are a real princess. No other person could be quite so sensitive."

"I knew it the moment I saw you!" exclaimed the prince.

The king shook his head in bewilderment. "I don't understand. Does this mean we have a wedding to plan or not?" he asked, and everybody laughed.

The prince and the real princess were married a month later, and lived very happily ever after. The pea was placed in the palace museum for all to see. In fact, unless someone has taken it, that's where you'll find it still.

THE EMPEROR'S NEW CLOTHES

As usual, the emperor was admiring himself in the mirror. "I really am a very stylish fellow, don't you think?" he asked his prime minister.

21

"But of course, Your Excellency," agreed the prime minister. "Everyone says you are the best dressed emperor in the entire world."

The emperor's mood suddenly changed. "But what am I going to do?" he wailed. "The royal parade is next week and I don't have a stitch to wear!"

The prime minister cast a confused glance around the room. There were new clothes strewn across the floor and draped over every piece of furniture. But, before he could speak, there came a knock at the door and a footman brought in two visitors.

"Who are you?" asked the emperor.

The newcomers bowed. "Your Excellency," said one of them, "we have come to offer you our services."

His partner stepped forward. "We make the most marvellous suits out of a very special cloth that we weave ourselves," he said.

"I have my own weavers and tailors," said the emperor. "What makes you think you're any better than them?"

"The world's most fashionable people all say our cloth is the most beautiful they've ever seen," boasted the first weaver.

"They also say you have the most excellent taste," added the other.

"But that's not all," continued the first. "Our cloth also has a unique quality that Your Excellency might find useful…"

"Our cloth is completely invisible to people who are too stupid to see it," the two weavers said together.

The emperor was amazed. "How extraordinary!" he cried. "I absolutely have to have a suit made from your wonderful cloth. Can you make one in time for my royal parade next week?"

"Certainly, Your Excellency," they replied, bowing again. "All we need is a place to work and an advance payment to cover our costs. Craftsmanship as specialized as ours doesn't come cheap."

"I don't care about the cost!" exclaimed the emperor. "Prime Minister, give these gentlemen whatever they need." Then he dismissed them all so he could decide what to wear for lunch.

The weavers were given two chests full of money, and a workshop in the palace grounds where they set up two large, wooden looms.

All through the night, the lights blazed from the weavers' windows. The emperor was desperate to see the cloth they were weaving, but all he could see was their silhouetted figures that seemed to be hard at work inside.

As the week went on, the emperor grew more and more curious about how the cloth was coming along. So he sent the prime minister to have a look.

When the prime minister arrived at the workshop, the weavers grinned broadly and invited him in to see their work. "Just look at this pattern," said one, pointing at his loom. "It's as fine and as intricate as a cobweb, don't you think?"

The prime minister stared at the loom,
his eyes widening in horror. "I don't believe it!"
he thought. "I can't see a single thread."

"See how these golden yellows shine as
brightly as the sun, and these blues shimmer like
the Arabian Sea," said the second weaver, with a
mischievous twinkle in his eye.

The prime minister rubbed his eyes and
looked again. But no matter how hard he stared,
he still couldn't see a thing. "I mustn't let anyone

know I can't see the cloth," he thought. "If the emperor thinks I am stupid, I'll lose my job."

"You're very quiet," said one of the men. "Don't you like it?"

"Oh, er, well, I'm no expert, but I'm sure the emperor will be very pleased with it," said the prime minister, stumbling over his words. "Anyway, royal parade to prepare for, no time to talk!" And with that he hurried off.

The emperor was pacing back and forth when the prime minister arrived back at the throne room. "Well, did you see it?" he demanded. "How does it look?"

"Er, well, Your Excellency, it's like nothing I've ever seen," he said, staring shiftily at his feet.

"Good, good. But tell me what it looks like," the emperor pressed eagerly.

"Er, well… It has a pattern… as intricate as a cobweb. The yellows shine like the sun, and the blues shimmer like the sea," the prime minister began hesitantly. "Your new outfit will look quite beyond compare," he concluded.

The emperor clapped his hands in delight. He was really looking forward to the royal parade now. And he wasn't the only one. By this time, word had spread about the emperor's new suit that would be invisible to people who were too stupid to see it. The whole city buzzed with excitement.

Two days before the parade, the emperor decided to send another official to find out how the cloth was coming along. This time he chose his second-most important and trusted advisor – his tailor.

When he was shown the looms, the tailor squinted through his spectacles. "Goodness, I can't see a thing!" he exclaimed. "But I am rather short-sighted," he added hastily.

"Please, come and take a closer look," urged one of the weavers.

"In your professional opinion, isn't it the most uniquely beautiful cloth you've ever seen?" asked the other.

The tailor peered in closer, but he still couldn't see a single stitch of thread. Bewildered, he took off his spectacles, wiped them with his handkerchief and put them back on again. But he still couldn't see anything on the looms.

"I'll lose my job if I let anyone know that I can't see this cloth." he realized in a panic. So to the weavers he said, "I can see that you are clearly masters of your craft." Then he rushed back to tell the emperor.

"Well?" asked the emperor excitedly. "How does it look?"

"Your Excellency, there are no words to describe the incredible beauty of the cloth." the tailor said awkwardly. "In my professional opinion, it is utterly unique."

"I'm going to look fabulous in my new suit!" crowed the emperor, dancing with glee.

The next morning, the weavers sent the emperor a message to say that the cloth was finished. They invited him to come and see it so they could measure him for his suit.

Without a moment's hesitation, the emperor raced across the palace grounds with his advisors straggling behind him. When he arrived at the workshop he was flushed and breathless.

The weavers bowed and held open the door for him. "Your Excellency, how marvellous to see you," they said. "Please come in."

"Though I say so myself, it really is our best work yet," said one of them, as he showed the emperor the looms.

"Don't you think it's the most beautiful cloth you've ever seen?" asked the other.

The emperor's jaw dropped as he stared in dismay. He couldn't see a thing on either of the looms. "It's—" he faltered.

"Delightful?" suggested the tailor.

"Magnificent?" added the prime minister.

For a moment, the other officials looked on in awkward silence, each wondering whether he was the only one who couldn't see the cloth.

But none of them wanted to admit that he couldn't see anything, so soon they all joined the prime minister and the tailor with cries of, "Wonderful!" "Glorious!" and "Divine!"

The emperor stared and stared, but he still couldn't see the cloth. "I don't believe it!" he thought. "Am I the only person here too stupid to see the cloth? This is the worst thing that has ever happened to me."

To hide his embarrassment, the emperor finally declared, "It's absolutely splendid. I love it!" And then, holding out his arms, he said, "Measure me up. I want this suit to fit me perfectly tomorrow."

"Certainly, Your Excellency," replied one of the weavers, taking out his measuring tape.

"Naturally, we will need some more money for needles and pins, buttons and trimmings, to finish off the outfit," added the other, as he wrote down the emperor's measurements.

"Of course, of course. I'll have it sent to you immediately," agreed the emperor, and he left them to get on with their work.

All through the night, the lights blazed in the windows of the weavers' workshop so everyone could see their silhouetted figures working away. They cut shapes out of the air with huge scissors and sewed with needles but no thread.

The next day, the emperor woke up just before dawn, filled with nervous excitement. He paced up and down his dressing room waiting for the weavers to bring him his new suit.

After what seemed like hours, they finally arrived carrying a large leather chest and looking very pleased with themselves. "Your suit is ready," they announced.

"Well, what are you waiting for?" cried the emperor, "Help me into my new clothes."

So the two men opened up the chest, pretending to pull out different articles of clothing and put them on the emperor.

"Here is your shirt," said one. "The cloth is so light, it's almost like having nothing on at all."

"And these are your trousers," said the other trickster. "Just look at the pattern of rich reds, deep purples and gold pinstripes."

"Well, how do I look?" the emperor asked.

"So stylish," the tailor cooed.

"Most majestic," the prime minister gushed.

The weavers tied an imaginary cloak around the emperor's shoulders then stood back to admire their work. "The suit fits you perfectly!" they said.

"You'll look so splendid at this parade that people will talk about it for years to come."

Outside the palace, the city streets were packed with cheering crowds, eager to see the emperor's new clothes. People were waving flags from their windows and some had even climbed into the trees to get a good view.

With a grand fanfare, the emperor and his advisors emerged from the palace. Everyone gasped. Then someone shouted, "Three cheers for the emperor's new clothes!" and the crowd whooped with delight. Of course, nobody could see a thing, but not one person would admit it.

Very soon, the streets were ringing with a chorus of praise for the emperor's amazing new suit. "The suit is so well cut," cried one onlooker.

"What stunning cloth," exclaimed another.

"The train is superb," added a third.

The emperor beamed with pride. "This is my

most popular outfit ever," he thought, and he marched down the stairs from the palace with an extra spring in his step.

Standing at the back of the crowd, a little boy tugged at his father's coat. "Father, please can you lift me up so I can see?"

The father lifted his son on to his shoulders. As soon as he could see the emperor, the little boy squealed in surprise. "The emperor's got no clothes on!" he piped up.

The crowd fell silent. Then the boy's father whispered to his wife, "The boy's right, you know. The emperor really is stark naked."

A woman nearby overheard them and whispered to the person next to her. Like wildfire, the whisper spread though the crowd. The whisper grew to a murmur and the murmur

swelled to a roar. In no time, the entire crowd was chanting, "The emperor's got no clothes on!"

The emperor looked down at himself. "They're right," he realized and he blushed from his head to his toes. "But what choice do I have but to keep going? This is a royal parade, and I am the emperor." So he held his head high and marched on.

"This is the best royal parade ever!" cried the little boy. Everyone agreed with him, and they cheered even louder than before.

In all the excitement, no one noticed the tricksters slip away through the back streets, their bags stuffed with the emperor's money. They were never seen again, but one thing they had said did turn out to be true. People really did talk about the emperor's parade for years to come.

THUMBELINA

There was once a woman who longed
for a daughter. But there was no room
in her little house for an ordinary-sized
child. "She would have to be really tiny
– no bigger than my thumb,"
the woman said.

She had no idea how she could get such a tiny child, so she went to visit a witch who lived nearby and explained what she wanted.

"That's easy," said the witch. She rummaged around in her storeroom and came back with a tiny seed. "Take this and plant it in a flowerpot," she said, "and you shall see what you shall see."

The woman pressed a coin into the witch's hand and hurried home. As soon as she had planted the seed, a shoot sprang up. Before her very eyes it grew into a flower bud, with scarlet petals all tightly pressed together.

"How beautiful!" the woman exclaimed. She leaned forward and gave the bud a kiss. At once the petals sprang open with a loud "Pop!"

Inside the flower sat the tiniest, loveliest girl the woman had ever seen.

"My dream has come true," she declared. "You aren't even as big as my thumb. I think I'll call you Thumbelina. Come on then, Thumbelina, let's see what fun we can have."

She filled a shallow dish with water and set it down on a table. Then she floated a tulip petal on the water like a little boat, and found two splinters for oars. Thumbelina climbed on board and spent all afternoon rowing back and forth across the miniature lake, singing happily.

At dinnertime, Thumbelina ate crumbs from the woman's plate, and at night, she slept in a polished walnut shell.

It had sweet-smelling violet petals for a mattress and a velvety rose petal for a blanket, and rocked gently to and fro just like a cradle.

One night, as Thumbelina was sleeping peacefully in her walnut shell, a big toad crept in through an open window and hopped down onto the table beside her. "What a beautiful little girl," croaked the toad. "She would make a perfect wife for my son." And she picked up the cradle in her mouth and hopped away into the night.

Thumbelina awoke the next morning to find herself on a lily pad in the middle of a stream, with a pair of huge, warty toads looking down at her.

"Hello Wife!" one of them croaked, and she jumped right out of her walnut shell in fright.

"Don't worry," the mother toad laughed, "you'll soon get used to the idea of marrying my son. In the meantime, I will get your bedroom ready." She picked up the walnut bed and swam off with it to the edge of the river.

The toad's son beamed at Thumbelina. "I'll come back for you later, my sweetheart," he croaked, and swam off after his mother. Thumbelina sat down on the lily pad and burst into tears.

The golden fishes in the stream were curious to see who the toad's wife was to be, and they poked their heads out of the water to look. "She's too pretty to be a toad's wife," said one.

"She doesn't look too happy about it either," said another.

"Let's help her," said a third. So the fishes gathered around the lily pad and nibbled through its stem to set Thumbelina free.

"Goodbye, sweet girl," they called, as the lily pad floated away downstream. "We hope you find better fortune elsewhere."

Thumbelina cheered up as she drifted along. The river rippled gold in the sunlight, and birds sang sweetly from the trees on either side. Thumbelina gazed at the shore as it slipped by, and wondered where she would end up next.

Soon a pretty white butterfly
came fluttering past. It liked the
look of Thumbelina and landed
on the lily pad.

"Perhaps you'd like to pull me
along?" said Thumbelina, and she tied one
end of her ribbon belt around the butterfly's
furry body and fastened the other end to the lily
pad. The butterfly fluttered its wings and took
off. It pulled her happily downstream for a while.

Suddenly a loud buzzing filled the air, and an
enormous cockchafer beetle flew down and
snatched Thumbelina from the lily pad. "Please
stop!" she cried as they lurched up into the air.
She was terrified of the beetle, but even more
worried for her new friend. "At least let me
untie the poor butterfly," she begged.

But the beetle took no notice,
and the butterfly fluttered off down
the stream still tied to the lily pad.

The cockchafer flew to a high treetop and put
Thumbelina down on a leaf. "I think you're pretty,
so I'm going to keep you," it told her in its strange,
creaky voice.

It called to its friends, and they all came
buzzing along to look at Thumbelina. She shivered
with fear as the huge black insects gathered around
and stared at her. One of them prodded her in the
back with its claw.

"Isn't she pretty?" the cockchafer said proudly.

"Not at all!" said one of the others. "She's far too skinny around the middle, instead of being nice and round like us."

"And she only has two legs," scoffed another. "Where are the other four?"

The cockchafer stared at Thumbelina. "You're right," he agreed. He grasped the tiny girl around the waist and flew down to the ground. "I don't want you after all," he told her. "You're too ugly." And he flew away again.

Thumbelina eyes filled with tears. "What will become of me now?" she thought. Then she dried her face on her skirt. "There's no point in crying about it," she said to herself.
"I must find what I need to survive."

She found a shelter under a pair of burdock leaves, and wove a grass hammock to hang between them.

All summer long she lived there. When she was hungry she ate berries from the hedges; when she was thirsty she sipped nectar from wild flowers.

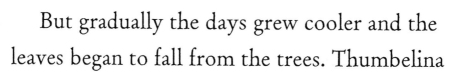

But gradually the days grew cooler and the leaves began to fall from the trees. Thumbelina shivered in her grass hammock, and couldn't find anything to keep her warm. So she set out to find somewhere to shelter for the winter.

Just as she started off, it began to snow. Poor Thumbelina! She was so tiny that every snowflake that landed on her was the same as a shovelful of snow landing on a normal-sized person.

She struggled into a cornfield that had been harvested of its corn. Only the stalks were left, which were as tall as trees to Thumbelina.

After a long walk through the stalk forest, she came to a little doorway. She knocked on the door, and a friendly, whiskered face appeared. It was a field mouse. "You look frozen," the mouse squeaked. "Come inside to warm up."

It was very snug inside the mouse's hole, and there was plenty of corn to eat. "You may stay all winter if you like," said the field mouse.

Thumbelina was very grateful. Over the next few days, she kept the little home neat and tidy, and sang songs to entertain the mouse.

One morning the mouse said, "My friend the mole is coming to visit today. He lives next door, and comes once a week. He's very kind – he might even marry you if you're lucky. Only don't speak too fondly of flowers or sunshine, as he doesn't like them. Try to show an interest in worms and the dark if you can..."

Later on, the mole came to call. He dug a tunnel through the mouse's wall and climbed into the room, brushing the soil off his dark, velvety fur.

The mouse introduced him to Thumbelina and they all chatted pleasantly for a while.

Then the mouse asked Thumbelina, "Why don't you sing a song for our guest?" So she did. She sang very beautifully, and the mole, while he listened, quietly fell in love with her.

When he was going home, the mole turned to the mouse and said, "I'll leave the tunnel open, so you can both come and see me whenever you like. I'll show you the way to my house now, if you'll follow me."

He crawled into the hole and called back over his shoulder. "Don't be afraid of the dead bird lying in the tunnel. It fell in while I was digging."

Thumbelina and the mouse followed the mole into the tunnel and saw a lovely swallow, with soft, blue feathers and closed eyes.

Thumbelina felt terribly sorry for him. "He must have died of the cold," she said.

"Foolish thing," said the mole. "I'm glad my children won't be birds. All they do is sing and then die of cold."

"Quite right," the mouse agreed.

Thumbelina didn't answer, but when the mouse and the mole had turned their backs, she stroked the swallow's feathers and kissed his soft head. "I think I heard your song last summer," she whispered. "I was very glad of it."

Later that night, she couldn't sleep for thinking of the poor swallow. She took the leaf that she was using as a bed cover, crept back into the tunnel, and laid it gently over the creature. Then she sat down beside him and stroked his head.

"I can't bear to think of you lying here all cold and alone," she said. She laid her head on

his downy breast. To her surprise, she felt a very faint heartbeat against her cheek. The swallow was alive!

Thumbelina rushed back to the mouse's hole and gathered together all the warm bedding she could find. Then she came back and wrapped it around the swallow. Lying down beside him, she wrapped her little arms around his body.

As morning broke, she felt the swallow stirring. He opened his eyes and looked at her. "Thank you," he whispered weakly.

Thumbelina brought him dew in a leaf to drink, and fed him little pieces of corn.

The swallow told her that he had been preparing to fly to a warmer country for the winter, as he did every year, when he had hurt one of his wings on a thorn bush. All the other swallows had flown away and he had stayed behind in the cold until he couldn't remember any more.

Day after day, Thumbelina nursed the swallow. He grew stronger and his wing healed. Neither the mouse nor the mole would have anything to do with the bird. When spring came, Thumbelina scratched a hole in the ceiling of the tunnel, and helped her friend climb out into the sunshine.

"I owe you my life," the swallow said to Thumbelina. "I hope one day I can repay you." He stretched out his soft blue wings and fluttered up into the sky.

Thumbelina watched him go with tears in her eyes and turned back into the dark tunnel.

That very day, the mole asked her to marry him. "When the nasty summer is over, we'll have our wedding," he said. And the mouse clapped his hands in glee.

When Thumbelina confessed privately to the mouse that she didn't love the mole, the creature frowned. "You ungrateful thing. Do you think I'm going to feed you forever? The mole is a good creature and will look after you. If you say no to him, I will throw you out of my house."

Preparations began for the wedding. The mouse asked the spiders to weave Thumbelina a silken dress, and the mole spoke to her tenderly of the days they would spend in his dark burrow. "And you need never go out into

the horrible sunshine again, my darling," he
said happily.

Poor Thumbelina's heart sank. She loved the
sunshine and the flowers, and would miss the
birdsong and the sky terribly if she married the
mole. But what choice did she have?

The day before her wedding, towards the end
of the summer, Thumbelina went outside to bid
a sad goodbye to the sun. "I wonder where the
swallow is now," she said gazing up at the sky.
"I wish I could have flown away with him."

"Tweet-tweet!" came a call above her, and a
bird swooped down and landed on the ground
beside her. It was the swallow.

"Did I hear you correctly?" he asked.
"If you really want to fly away, then come with
me. I am flying south for the winter, to a land

where it never snows or gets cold. You could live there very happily I think. I'll take you there on my back, if you like."

Thumbelina threw her arms around the bird's neck. "There's nothing I'd like more!" she said. She hopped on the swallow's back right there and then and he soared into the air.

Thumbelina laughed with joy as the breeze blew through her hair. She looked up to the sunlit sky and felt freer than she ever had before.

The tiny girl was as light as a feather so the swallow had no trouble carrying her on his journey. They flew across deep, green forests and snow-topped mountains, and then over the sparkling sea.

After a while, Thumbelina grew sleepy. She snuggled into the swallow's downy feathers

and fell fast asleep.

When she awoke, they had arrived in another land. The hills below them shone gold in the light of the warm sun, and as they swooped lower, Thumbelina could see lemons and oranges growing on the trees.

They flew on until they reached a beautiful white marble palace at the edge of a blue lake. "This is my house," said the swallow. "If you like, you could live in a flower in the garden." He landed by a group of pretty pink flowers, and Thumbelina stepped off his back onto one of them. She sat down in its soft middle. "This would be a lovely home," she said in delight.

"It already is," said a quiet voice.

Thumbelina turned around to find a man not much bigger than herself standing in the middle of the flower. He had pale skin and fair hair, and wore a little golden crown on his head.

"I'm sorry," gasped Thumbelina. "I didn't mean to intrude."

The little man smiled warmly at her. "Not at all," he said. "I am king of the flower fairies. You're welcome to stay here with me."

He took the crown from his head and placed it on Thumbelina's.

"In fact," he said, "would you like to be queen of all the flower fairies? That is to say, will you marry me?"

Thumbelina had fallen in love with him right on the spot. So she said, "Yes!" with all her heart.

All the other fairies welcomed Thumbelina as one of their own. When she told them her name, they said she was much too pretty for it, and so they gave her a flower fairy name instead. From that moment she was known as 'Maia'.

The wedding was held among the flowers. The swallow sang for them, and the fairies brought all kinds of wonderful gifts. Best of all was a pair of delicate wings for Thumbelina. With them, she could fly from flower to flower, just like the flower fairies.

The swallow flew back home that summer, as he did every year. He landed in a tree outside a window, and he sang all about this story.

It just so happened that a man was sitting inside the window. The man was a teller of fairy tales. He listened very carefully to the story and wrote it all down. And that's how we know about it today.

THE UGLY DUCKLING

One by one, the little ducklings broke out of their eggs. Their mother watched proudly as they fluffed up their yellow feathers and took their first eager steps into the big wide world. But there was one egg that still hadn't hatched.

"Oh dear!" said the mother duck. "I wonder why it's taking so long."

Just then, the old duck from down the lane waddled by. When she saw the egg, she shook her head and tut-tutted. "It looks like you've got a turkey's egg there," she said. "I'd leave it alone if I were you."

The mother duck looked worried. "I think I'll just wait a few more days," she said.

She waited and waited. Then, at last, there was a tap, tap, tap and a beak broke through the shell. Slowly, a strange, straggly creature struggled out of the egg. He was much bigger than the other ducklings and had dull, grubby-looking feathers.

"Come along," said the mother duck, nudging him with her beak. "Follow me."

The little ducklings all hurried after her
in a line, with the newcomer tottering along
awkwardly at the back.

When they came to the
pond, the mother duck
jumped into the water.
One after the other, the
ducklings plopped in
behind her until only
the big duckling was left.

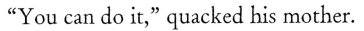

"You can do it," quacked his mother.

The duckling looked doubtful, but then he
took a deep breath and jumped into the water.
A moment later, he bobbed to the surface, his
webbed feet paddling furiously. "You *can* swim,"
his mother beamed. "A turkey indeed! What
does that silly old duck know?"

On the way home, the mother duck took her brood through the farmyard to show them off. As they passed, the hens nudged one another and pointed. "Look at the state of that duckling," they clucked. "Have you ever seen anything so ugly? It looks like a turkey chick."

"That hideous creature a relative of mine? What an absurd idea!" spluttered the turkey.

"You're not exactly an oil painting yourself, you know," muttered one of the hens, and the others all cackled loudly.

This really ruffled the turkey's feathers. Turning red in the face, he puffed himself up and chased after the duckling. "Get out of here," he gobbled furiously. "You're not welcome."

The poor duckling tried to get away, but in his hurry he tripped and fell flat on his beak.

The hens screeched with laughter. "Look how clumsy he is," they jeered. "Anyone can see he doesn't belong here."

"Go away! Go away!" cheeped their chicks, pecking at him spitefully.

The ugly duckling ran this way and that, but everywhere he turned there were cruel beaks and mocking faces. In a flurry of feathers, he fled from the farmyard.

He ran until darkness fell around him. Then he crept into the bushes and hid his head under his wing.

In the morning, the duckling was woken by a strange honking sound. He peeked out of the bushes and found two wild geese staring at him.

"What on earth do you think that is?" asked the first goose.

"I really can't tell," replied the second.

The duckling shrank back, trembling. "Don't worry," said the first goose. "We won't hurt you."

"Of course not," chuckled the other. "You're a funny little thing, but I rather like you. Why don't you come with us?"

Before the duckling could reply, there was a loud bang right by them. The geese flew into a panic. "Help! Help! The hunters are here," they cried. They took flight and left the duckling sitting all alone.

A moment later a hunting dog splashed through the reeds, growling and baring its teeth.

Too terrified to move, the duckling closed his eyes tightly and waited for the dog to snap him up. But the dog took one look at him and then turned and ran back.

The duckling opened his eyes and breathed a sigh of relief. "Luckily I'm so ugly that even the dog won't come near me," he thought. Yet in his heart he felt sad and lonely.

He waited until the gunshots had died down and went on his way. Soon, it started to rain. The duckling got soaking wet and looked more bedraggled than ever.

Eventually, he came to a ramshackle barn. The door was hanging off its hinges and the roof looked ready to fall in, but at least it was dry.

The duckling crept inside and huddled in a corner. A cat happened to be taking shelter there too, and watched him silently from the rafters. Then it leaped down, and prowled around the duckling, staring at him with glinting green eyes. "What sort of creature are you?" it asked suspiciously.

"I'm not sure," replied the duckling.

"Not sure?" repeated the cat. Its ears twitched and its eyes narrowed. "Well, let's see. Can you purr?" it asked.

"No," said the duckling.

"Can you swish your tail?" said the cat, flicking its tail menacingly.

"I'm afraid not," answered the duckling.

"Can you arch your back?" asked the cat.

The duckling shook his head.

"Well, what can you do?" asked the cat.

The duckling thought for a moment and then proudly declared, "I can swim!"

The cat shuddered. "Sssssswim," it hissed in disgust. "Why would anybody want to do a thing like that?"

"You wouldn't understand," said the duckling miserably. "I think I'd better be on my way."

So he set out into the world again, but wherever he went it was just the same. Frogs hopped out of his way, squirrels nudged one another as he waddled by, and storks stared down their beaks at him.

Eventually, the duckling hid himself away in long reeds around a lake, where nobody could see him to make unkind remarks.

Then, one evening, just as the sun was setting, there was a rustle among the reeds and a flock of beautiful birds sailed out onto the lake. Their feathers were dazzling white and they had long, slender necks. They were swans.

Suddenly, they began to run across the water, beating their mighty wings. The duckling watched in awe as they flew up into the sky. "Please don't go!" he cried. But the swans were already too far away to hear him.

The ugly duckling felt lonelier than ever. The wind swept through the trees, stripping the golden leaves from their branches. A raven swooped down and settled on a bare branch. "Winter's coming," it croaked gloomily.

The weather grew colder and colder. Snowflakes drifted down from the sky and ice crept across the surface of the lake. It became harder and harder to find food.

The hungry duckling climbed out of the lake and wandered around in the forest looking for something to eat. Evening fell and long blue shadows stretched across the ground. The snow looked so soft that he lay down and fell asleep.

In the morning, a woodcutter found him there, cold and stiff. Gently, the man picked up the creature and carried it home.

The woodcutter laid the ugly duckling down
by the fire, and his children gathered around it.
When the ugly duckling woke up to find their
curious faces staring down at him, he was so
frightened that he flapped around the kitchen
and knocked over a milk jug.

The children laughed and ran after him,
wanting to play. In a panic, the duckling flapped
up out of their way, but this time he landed in
a jar of flour.

"Look at the mess you've made," scolded
the woodcutter's wife. "Get out of here!"

Leaving a trail of floury footprints behind
him, the duckling ran out of the door. His
webbed feet padded along faster and faster. He
beat his wings, and a moment later found himself
soaring up into the sky.

He flew and flew until he
felt the gentle warmth of the
sun on his wings. In the
meadow where he landed,
the snow had begun to
melt and snowdrops were
peeking through.

Little by little, the land turned green again.
Bees buzzed from flower to flower and the larks
sang a welcome each morning. It was spring.

One day, the ugly duckling was swimming
on a lake when he saw three swans. He wanted
to rush out to greet them, but he hesitated. They
were so elegant and he was so ugly that he hardly
dared to approach them.

Then he thought, "What have I got to lose?"
Plucking up his courage, he swam to meet them.

When the swans saw him, they rushed towards him with their wings outstretched.

The duckling cowered from them, thinking they were going to beat him. But they didn't. They bowed their heads politely instead, and said, "Welcome to the lake. It's always nice to meet one of our kind."

"What do you mean?" said the duckling in confusion. "I'm not at all like you. I'm brown and ugly..."

One of the swans smiled and said, "Not any more. Have you seen yourself recently? Take a look in the water."

The duckling looked down at his reflection and gasped. His curved neck was long and elegant, and all his feathers were dazzling white. He wasn't an ugly duckling any longer.

"I'm a swan!" he cried. "I'm a beautiful swan!" From that moment on, he was the happiest swan that ever lived.

THE LITTLE MERMAID

Deep beneath the ocean lay an extraordinary
palace. Its walls were made of delicate coral,
the roof was adorned with pretty shells,
and jewel-bright fish darted in and out
of the open windows.

The palace belonged to the king of the sea, who lived there with his six daughters. The princesses were all very beautiful, with long, wavy hair and shimmering tails. But the youngest was the most beautiful of all. Her eyes were bluer than the ocean itself and her skin was whiter than pearls.

Yet it was the youngest princess's voice that really made her stand out from the others. When she sang, it was as though a thousand silvery bells were echoing throughout the ocean.

The princesses led a happy and carefree life. The sea creatures were their playmates. All day long, they played hide-and-seek together among the coral. They took rides on turtles' backs, danced with the octopuses and laughed at the clownfishes' funny antics.

But most of all they loved to hear about the world beyond the waves. The princesses would listen, spellbound, as their grandmother told stories of mermaids without tails, flying fish that could sing and starfish that twinkled in the night sky. Her granddaughters had never seen people or birds or stars, so this was how she described them so that they could understand.

The princesses couldn't wait to see it all. "When you turn fifteen, you shall," promised their grandmother.

"That seems like forever," sighed the youngest princess, who had the longest to wait.

While her sisters played, she would often wander in the palace garden, dreaming about the world above. She sniffed the flowers and tried to imagine the sweet scent of the flowers on land.

The other princesses had made flower beds in the shapes of sea creatures, but hers was round like the sun. In the middle was a marble statue of a young man that she had found on the seabed. She would sit and gaze at it for hours on end.

Eventually, the eldest princess's fifteenth birthday arrived. "Don't worry," she told her sisters as they waved goodbye. "I'll come back soon and tell you all about it."

The princesses waited impatiently for her to return. At one point, they heard a splash and dashed outside, but it was just a turtle.

When at last she came back, they crowded around. "What did you see?" they asked eagerly.

"I lay on a beach in the moonlight, and watched the twinkling lights of the town," she said dreamily. "The church bells chimed across the bay, so much brighter and clearer than the muffled sounds of the ocean."

The Little Mermaid closed her eyes and tried to imagine the bells ringing. She longed to hear them for herself.

It was a whole year before it was the second sister's turn to visit the world above. She emerged as the sun was setting, just in time to witness a flock of swans flying across the red-gold sky.

"I've never seen such majestic creatures," she told her sisters. "They were so strong and yet so graceful."

The third sister's birthday was in winter time, and when she reached the surface she had to break through the sea ice. Icebergs towered above her, sparkling like diamonds as the sun shone through them.

The fourth sister was the boldest, so when her time came, she decided to explore further inland. She swam up a river and between some green hills until she reached a pretty lake where some children were splashing around.

At first, she thought they were mermaids too. Then she noticed they had no tails and realized they must be people.

She swam towards them, but a great, hairy

creature ran at her, making a terrible noise. It was only a dog, but the princess had never seen or heard one before, so she turned tail and fled.

Her sisters listened to her story with awe. The world above the ocean sounded like a wonderful, terrifying place.

After hearing about this adventure, the fifth sister wasn't taking any chances. She stayed out on the open sea, where she saw whales spouting fountains of water and dolphins leaping into the air. "I'm sure it's just as beautiful as the land, and much safer," she declared when she returned.

Her older sisters nodded. Now that they'd seen the world for themselves, they were quite content to stay at home in the sea kingdom.

But the youngest princess was still desperate to explore the world above.

Every night, she stared out of her window at the dark blue water and tried to picture the moon shining in the starry sky.

At long last, the Little Mermaid's turn came. She rose through the water like a bubble, up and up and up. Bursting onto the surface, she took a deep breath. The fresh, salty air made her tongue tingle.

As she looked up, she gasped. Looming above her was a huge ship with tall masts. Strings of lanterns swung as it dipped on the water and lively music drifted down on the breeze.

The Little Mermaid bobbed eagerly on the waves, trying to see what was happening. Up on deck, there were people dancing. Ladies in bright silk ballgowns whirled around, accompanied by gentlemen in tall hats and fancy waistcoats.

Then a trumpet sounded and a handsome young man appeared. Everyone turned towards him. The gentlemen bowed and the ladies curtsied, for the young man was a prince and today was his birthday.

The Little Mermaid was so enthralled that she didn't notice the weather start to change. Waves chased across the ocean and seagulls circled the mast, shrieking a warning. But no one listened.

Then the sky darkened and large drops of rain began to fall. The wind struck up, and the guests hurried for cover, but the prince stayed to help the crew. Sailors ran to and fro, unfurling the ship's sails, which flapped in the wind like startled birds.

The sea grew wild and angry. Waves crashed across the deck and tossed the ship from side to side. Thunder rolled and lightning bolts ripped through the sky.

With a mighty crack, the mast snapped in two and smashed down onto the deck. The ship gave a mournful groan and slowly keeled over.

The Little Mermaid saw the prince plunge into the sea. For a moment, her heart leaped at the thought that he would be with her. But then she remembered that her grandmother had once told her that people couldn't live underwater.

Quickly, she swam towards the prince through the splintered wreckage, but before she could reach him he sank beneath the waves. With a flick of her tail, the Little Mermaid dived after him. She held tightly on to him and swam to the surface.

The prince's eyes were closed but he was still breathing. Close up, he looked just like the statue in her garden at home, and the Little Mermaid fell in love with him.

All night long she held the prince in her arms. Carefully, she kept his head above the water and let the restless waves carry them along.

By the time the sun's rays crept across the sky in the morning, she was exhausted, but at last the sea was calm. The waves had carried them into a sheltered cove lined with palm trees.

The Little Mermaid laid the prince on the warm sand. Pushing his wet hair out of his eyes, she kissed him gently on the forehead.

Just then, a noise disturbed her. Slipping back into the sea, she hid behind a rocky outcrop.

A pretty young girl appeared and hurried

over to the prince. He opened his eyes and smiled at her gratefully, for he did not know that it was the Little Mermaid who had rescued him. The girl smiled back and took hold of his hand.

The Little Mermaid couldn't bear to watch any more. With a final, sorrowful glance, she dived beneath the waves.

Her sisters were waiting for her at the palace, eager to hear about what she had seen, but she refused to tell them anything.

As the weeks went by, she became more and more melancholy. Her hair grew tangled and her eyes lost their sparkle. Every day, she would sit by the statue in the garden and think about the prince, while the garden she had tended so lovingly turned into a wilderness.

Eventually, her grandmother took her aside.

"What's wrong, my dear?" she asked gently. "You were so much looking forward to seeing the world and yet since you returned you've been desperately sad."

The Little Mermaid sighed and told her all about the prince. "Isn't there any way I can live on land so that I could be near him?" she asked.

"It's not impossible..." her grandmother began. Then she stopped and shook her head. "You must forget about it," she said. "Things are different there. Your lovely tail would seem ugly to him. People think you need to walk on clumsy legs to be beautiful. You wouldn't be happy."

But the Little Mermaid couldn't forget. She'd heard her grandmother talk about a sea witch, and so she decided to ask her for help. The Little Mermaid felt sure the witch would know about such things, for she lived in a mangrove forest which stood half in the sea and half on the land.

It was a long way away and the Little Mermaid didn't know how to get there, so she asked a pilot fish to be her guide.

On the way, they passed the wreck of the prince's ship, and the Little Mermaid caught sight of the captain's skeleton. His bony fingers were still clutching the tiller. She shivered and swam quickly on.

The pilot fish led her around swirling whirlpools. They threatened to suck them into the very depths of the ocean where strange chimneys belch out clouds of black water and fish have lights so they can see one another in the dark.

Eventually, they came to the sea witch's mangrove forest. The pilot fish waited at the edge, leaving the Little Mermaid to go on alone.

As she dodged through the labyrinth of tangled roots, googly eyes peered out of the mud and eerie jellyfish floated by.

A sea snake glided up and coiled around her. "Come this way," it hissed. It led the Little Mermaid to the witch's cave. Taking a deep breath, she slipped inside.

"I know what you want," said the sea witch. Her piercing green eyes seemed to stare right into the Little Mermaid's heart. "I can prepare a potion that will enable you to walk on land, but it will hurt more than you can imagine."

"I'm not afraid," said the Little Mermaid, though her voice trembled as she spoke.

"You should be," said the sea witch. "Once you set foot on land, there's no going back. You can never return to your father's kingdom alive. If the prince falls in love with you, you will gain a human soul and live happily on land. But if he chooses to marry another, you will lose your life before the sun sets on their wedding day."

The Little Mermaid turned pale, but she thought of the prince and nodded. "I'll do it," she said.

"Very well," said the sea witch. She threw a handful of shark's teeth into her cauldron, added a few drops of blue blood from a squid and squeezed in the breath of a pufferfish.

Then she mixed it all together, chanting as she did. When the potion was ready, she poured it into a bottle.

The Little Mermaid reached out to take it, but the witch snatched it away. "You haven't paid me yet," she snarled.

"I don't have any money," said the princess.

"Then give me the most valuable thing you own," said the sea witch. "Your voice."

"B-but how will I talk to the prince?" stammered the Little Mermaid.

"That's no concern of mine," the witch snapped. "Do you want the potion or not?"

The Little Mermaid hesitated. "Yes," she whispered eventually. It was the last word she ever spoke.

She took the bottle and hurried back to the pilot fish. In silence, they swam up to the surface of the sea, and to the shore where the prince's palace was perched high on top of a cliff.

The Little Mermaid climbed onto the rocks and gazed up at the palace. Then she looked sorrowfully back out to sea. She blew a kiss to her family beneath the waves and swallowed the potion.

She felt a searing pain, as though a blazing sword had slashed through her tail, and when she looked down it was no longer there. In its place was a pair of fragile legs, which ended in two pretty white feet.

Cautiously, the Little Mermaid tried to stand, but the pain was agonizing. Her legs gave way and she fell to the ground. "Let me help you," said a warm voice. She looked up to see the prince holding out his hand.

Gratefully she took it, and together they climbed the winding stone staircase that led to the castle. Every step was like walking on knife edges, but the Little Mermaid endured it bravely.

"Where have you come from?" the prince asked her curiously, for she was draped only in a cloak of seaweed.

She tried to answer with her hands and her eyes, but the prince did not understand.

When the Little Mermaid had rested, the prince's servants dressed her in flowing robes of rich blue silk, embroidered with sparkling thread.

"You're beautiful," said the prince when he saw her, and the Little Mermaid blushed.

The two of them soon became close friends. The prince found her easy to talk to and told her his every secret. Of course, she never spoke a word in return, but her ocean-blue eyes were full of understanding.

One day, when they were walking in the palace gardens, the prince seemed distracted. "My father wants me to marry," he explained. "He has chosen a bride, and our wedding is tomorrow."

A tear rolled down the Little Mermaid's cheek. The prince wiped it away. "Don't cry for me with those wise eyes of yours," he said. "I'm sure I won't be forced to marry someone I don't love." He had no idea that the Little Mermaid was crying for herself.

That evening, beneath the mournful moon, the prince told stories of shipwrecks and mermaids, and the Little Mermaid listened sadly.

Suddenly he turned to her. He lifted her face towards his and gazed at it fondly. "I don't know why, but whenever I look at you it reminds me of someone," he said. "I was washed up on a beach and she rescued me. I only saw her once, but she captured my heart."

The Little Mermaid cried out silently inside, for she could not tell him the truth, that it was she who had saved his life.

In the morning, preparations for the prince's wedding party began. Bright banners were hung from the battlements, the chandeliers were dusted until they sparkled and the marble floors polished until they shone, while in the kitchens a grand banquet was being prepared. By the afternoon, the palace was ready for the royal wedding.

When the guests began to arrive, the band struck up a tune. "Let's dance," said the prince, and he swept the Little Mermaid into his arms.

As they floated across the floor, everyone was captivated by her graceful swaying movements.

The Little Mermaid danced as though her life depended on it. Her dainty feet were cut to ribbons, but in spite of the pain she wished the dance could last forever.

But, suddenly, the music stopped. A murmur went around the hall, and the prince's bride made her entrance. The prince stared in astonishment. "It's her," he gasped, for his bride was the girl who had found him on the beach.

From that moment on, the prince had eyes for no one else. He didn't notice the Little Mermaid creep away or the trail of footprints that led down to the sea.

Down on the shore, the Little Mermaid was bathing her feet. It stung terribly, but she also found the coolness strangely soothing.

She picked up a seashell and held it to her ear. For a moment, she thought she could hear her sisters calling to her.

As the sun sank down towards the horizon, the church bells rang out to celebrate the prince's wedding. They were even louder and clearer than the Little Mermaid had imagined. At the final chime, she slipped softly into the sea and dissolved in the deep blue waves.

THE EMPEROR AND THE NIGHTINGALE

The emperor of China had the most beautiful garden in all the world. It was full of delicate trees, trickling streams and sweet-scented flowers with silver bells on them that tinkled prettily in the breeze.

But even more wonderful than the garden, was the voice of a little bird that lived in it. The bird was a nightingale, and anyone who heard it sing was utterly delighted.

Maids stopped their chores to listen, gardeners leaned on their forks to enjoy the music, and visitors to the garden went home full of praise for the bird's song.

The emperor himself very rarely went into his garden. He didn't even know the bird existed.

One day, the emperor was reading a book all about his famous palace. He smiled proudly as he read how wonderful his garden was. But then he frowned. "It says here that the best thing in my garden is a nightingale that sings there," he said. "Where is this nightingale? I demand to hear it sing."

All the courtiers leaped into action. They ran
up and down staircases, and hurried along paths
and scurried across lawns looking for the
nightingale, but none of them could find it.

The truth was that none of them ever went
into the garden either, and they didn't have the
faintest idea what a nightingale was.

In the end a maid came to see what was going on. "Excuse me," she said timidly, "I can show you the nightingale. It sings to me every evening on my way home."

So the courtiers followed her through the garden to find the nightingale. On the way, they heard a sound in the distance. "Moo! Moo!"

"I can hear it!" one of the courtiers cried out in excitement. "What a marvellous song!"

"That's not the nightingale," said the maid. "That's a cow."

They passed by a pond and heard something else. "Croak! Croak!"

"I can hear it!" one of the courtiers called out. "What beautiful music!"

"That's not the nightingale," said the maid, trying not to laugh. "That's a frog."

Eventually they came to the trees where the nightingale lived. "There it is," said the maid, pointing to a little brown bird on a branch.

"That can't be it," said one of the courtiers. "How can such a dull-looking creature have a voice worth listening to?"

But the bird opened its little beak and began to sing. The music was so beautiful that by the time it had finished the courtiers were all weeping with pure happiness and blowing their noses.

"Dear nightingale," said the girl. "Our great emperor would very much like to hear you sing. Please will you come with us?"

The little brown bird flitted down from the

branch onto the maid's outstretched hand. "My song sounds better out here in the trees," it said, "but I will come."

When the nightingale was brought before the emperor, he looked disappointed. "That can't be it," he said. "How can such a drab creature be the best thing in my garden?" But then the bird opened its beak and began to sing.

By the time it had finished, the emperor was weeping with pure happiness and someone had to pass him a royal handkerchief to dry his eyes.

"You will have a golden cage to live in, right here in the palace, and you can sing to me all the time," he told the bird.

"Thank you but I have everything I need in the garden," said the bird.

But the emperor insisted, and so from then

on the bird had to live in a golden cage in the palace.

It looked out of the window longingly at the trees and the sky, but sang its best for the emperor every day.

More and more people came to the palace to hear the bird sing. The poor nightingale was exhausted with all the singing, and its voice grew thin and sad.

Then one day, the emperor received a gift. "A perfect nightingale for a perfect emperor," read the label. He unwrapped the gift to find a model of a nightingale with real jewels for eyes, real gold feathers and a little gold key to wind it up. "Splendid!" cried the emperor, clapping his hands. He wound the little key and the bird began to sing.

It had a plinky-plonky
metallic voice, and it moved
its metal head and blinked its
lifeless, jewel eyes. "This bird
will never grow tired of singing,"
the emperor said as he wound it up again.
"And it's so pretty to look at, too."

The emperor listened to the mechanical bird
a hundred times that day, and a hundred times
the next, and after three days everyone had
forgotten all about the real nightingale.

It flew away to live in the garden again,
regained its strength and its voice and was very
happy. So were the maids and the gardeners,
who loved to hear it sing.

Months went by and the emperor did almost
nothing but listen to his mechanical nightingale

sing. He listened to it when he woke up and again when he had breakfast, at lunch and after lunch and all afternoon. He invited people to dinner parties just to admire the wind-up bird.

But one morning when he wound up the bird, instead of singing, it said, "Click, click, whirr, clunk," and fell silent.

"It's broken!" cried the emperor. "Somebody fix it quick!"

All the courtiers leaped into action. They ran up and down staircases and all through the city, looking for someone to fix the nightingale.

The first craftsman they found opened the body, but he scratched his head when he saw the gold cogs and springs inside.

The second craftsman pulled the

cogs and springs out, but got
them all mixed up.

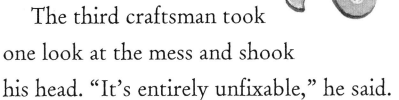

The third craftsman took
one look at the mess and shook
his head. "It's entirely unfixable," he said.

The emperor took to his bed with grief.
He kept the broken bird on his bedside table
and looked at it sadly. Nobody could make him
smile. He wouldn't eat and wouldn't drink and
grew pale and thin and ill.

Everybody crept around the palace fearfully,
thinking the emperor might die of misery.
Nobody had the slightest idea how to cheer
him up.

Then one morning the emperor heard a real
bird singing outside his window. Its beautiful,
warbling song lifted his heart.

"The nightingale!" he cried, jumping out of bed.

He looked out of the window and there was the little brown bird sitting on the branch of a tree.

"I heard you were ill," the nightingale said,

"so I thought I'd come and sing to try to make you feel better."

"I feel better already!" said the emperor. "I'm so sorry I ignored you. Will you come and live in the golden cage again, and sing for me every day?"

"I'd rather live out here, thank you all the same," said the nightingale. "But I do promise I'll come and sing for you every day."

From that moment on, the nightingale came and sang to the emperor once a day from the tree outside his window. The emperor forgot all about his broken mechanical bird. Instead, he walked more often in his beautiful garden, talked more often to his maids and gardeners, and lived a long and happy life.

THE FLYING TRUNK

The young man sighed as he looked up from the lines of figures in his accounts. "I don't think I'll bother counting all this money," he said, throwing down his quill pen. "I think it's safe to assume my father has left me enough to last my lifetime."

Sadly the young man had not
inherited his father's wisdom and he
soon began to fritter the money away. He tied
banknotes to kites and watched them float up
into the sky; he played tiddlywinks with silver
coins and laughed as they rolled into the gutter;
he bounced gold coins across the lake and
clapped when they plopped into the water.

The merchant's son made lots of new friends,
who were all full of ideas about how he should
spend his riches. He was so grateful for their
advice that he lavished them with gifts and threw
fabulous parties for them.

He bought his friends fancy suits and
flamboyant shirts with frilly collars,
and they rode to the opera in
horse-drawn carriages. For a time,

they enjoyed themselves immensely. But then one day the young man looked in the cellar and saw that there were only three chests of gold left. "Oh dear," he said, scratching his head. "Where can it all have gone? I'd better be more careful from now on."

He decided to change his ways. But no matter what he did, the young man never seemed to have any luck. He had a house built, and its foundations crumbled; he sent a ship to buy goods to sell, and it sank on the way home; he bet a sack full of gold on a racehorse, and it came in last.

As the young man's fortune disappeared, so did his friends. In desperation, he borrowed some money, but soon he lost all that too. Burly debt collectors came and carted away his belongings to repay what he owed.

Eventually, one of his more kind-hearted friends brought him a big old trunk. "You should pack up now, before you lose everything," he advised.

But by then it was too late. All the young man had left in the world was the dressing gown he was wearing. Feeling dejected, he climbed inside the trunk to try to think what to do next.

"I wish I was far away from all this," he muttered. The trunk began to judder and then suddenly lurched into the air. "Help!" cried the young man as it shot up the chimney. Up and up the trunk soared, high over the rooftops and into the sky. At first, he clung on tightly, not daring to look down. But, after a while, he grew more confident and peered down through the gaps in the clouds.

The sights that met his eyes filled him with wonder. The trunk flew over vast blue oceans where schools of dolphins leapt from the waves; it climbed over snow-capped mountains, soaring higher than the eagles; and it drifted over desert dunes, following the camel trains far below.

Eventually, the trunk swooped towards the ground. It crashed through the treetops, landing with a bump on the forest floor. The young man picked the leaves out of his hair and brushed himself down. Then he set off to explore.

He walked all day long until he came to a town, which lay in the shadow of a great castle. The gates of the castle were closed, the drawbridge was pulled up and it looked deserted. "Who does that castle belong to?" he asked a woman in the marketplace.

"The Sultan and Sultana live there with their daughter," the woman told him. "She is said to be very beautiful, but a wise man warned that her marriage is doomed, so her parents keep her hidden away in the highest tower of the castle."

This roused the young man's curiosity, so the next day he returned to his trunk. "Take me to the castle," he cried, and away they flew.

The trunk landed on the castle ramparts. Carefully, the young man climbed up the tower and slipped in through the window. The princess was lying asleep on a bed, her raven-black hair tumbling over the pillow. Overwhelmed by her beauty, he bent down and kissed her.

She woke up with a start and when she saw him she snatched up a veil and pulled it over her face, so that only her eyes were visible.

"Your eyes are like deep whirlpools," murmured the young man, "and your thoughts swim about in them like mermaids."

The princess blushed a delicate pink behind her veil. "Who are you?" she whispered. "And how did you get here?"

"I am an angel that flew down from the heavens to see you," he replied.

Then gently he lifted her veil and kissed her again. "Forgive my forwardness, but will you marry me?" he asked.

At this, the princess turned crimson. "You'll have to ask my parents," she said shyly. "But I'm afraid they will refuse."

The young man's face fell. "You're right," he said. "I have no money and no marriage gift to offer. They'll never agree to it."

They were both quiet for a moment. Then the princess said, "There may be a way to persuade them. They love stories, and nobody ever tells them any. If you told one they both really liked, they might just agree. But it won't be easy. My mother likes a tale with a moral, while my father prefers a story that will make him laugh."

The young man thought hard. "I know a good story," he said at last. "I'll tell it to them in the morning." He and the princess talked all night, and grew fonder and fonder of one another.

When morning came, the young man went to see the princess's parents. "I've come to ask for your daughter's hand in marriage," he declared.

The Sultan peered down his nose at the young man, who was still wearing his dressing gown and slippers. He seemed rather an unlikely suitor for a princess.

"I'm afraid I don't have anything to offer as a wedding gift," said the young man quickly, "except for the story in my head."

The Sultana raised her eyebrows. She couldn't resist a good story. "Let's hear it then," she said, and they settled down to listen.

The young man took a deep breath. "Once upon a time," he began, "there was a box of matches. They lived in a humble kitchen where their main purpose was to light the stove, but they often boasted about where they came from."

"We didn't always live like this," they told everyone. "We were born in the heart of the forest. Our father was a great old fir tree. He stood head and shoulders above the other trees. What a fine view we had."

"The other trees only dressed in green during the summer, but we wore emerald robes all year round," the matches bragged. "The dew sparkled like diamonds on our branches and the birds sounded a fanfare for us every morning."

"It sounds like a wonderful life," said the iron cooking pot. "Why did you leave it all behind?"

"It wasn't our choice," the matches sighed. "The woodcutter came and broke up our family. Our father got a position as the main mast of a ship in the royal navy, but we children were reduced to the mere splinters you see before you now."

"That must have been terrible," murmured the cooking pot sympathetically.

"What would you know about it?" said the matches haughtily. "You've seen nothing of the world outside."

"That's true enough, my dears," agreed the cooking pot. "I only know about life here in this kitchen. For as long as I can remember I've worked up a sweat from cooking all day long, and I've been scoured so much that I'm rough both inside and out."

The matches, who didn't think much of the cooking pot, muttered, "You can say that again."

At this, the Sultan guffawed. "Who are those matches to get so high and mighty?" he said.

"Hush," said the Sultana. "It's all very well laughing, but it's quite wrong for the matches to be so superior. Where's the moral in this tale?"

"Let's see if you find the moral you're looking for in the story's ending," said the young man, and he took up the tale again.

"I'm quite content here though," the cooking pot continued. "For me this has always been home. But kitchen life must seem very dull to you young things."

"Not at all," piped up the kettle. "We love your stories of everyday life in the kitchen. In fact, why don't you tell us some now?"

The cooking pot looked flustered. "I hardly know where to start," she said modestly.

"Tell us about when you first came home from the marketplace," begged the teaspoon, tapping on a cup to make everyone be quiet.

"Goodness me. It seems so long ago," said the cooking pot. "I was shiny and new, and I didn't have the faintest idea how to cook. My first stew was burned on the bottom, but the maid scrubbed me clean and everyone was very kind about it."

The cooking pot went on to recall the chilly winter mornings when the children hurried down for their porridge, and the excitement each day when they rushed home from school.

"They were so hungry that I always had to have their supper ready for them," she remembered fondly. "Then, afterwards, everyone used to huddle around the fire together. We had such happy times.

The kettle sighed. "It sounds so wonderfully homely," he said. The pans banged their lids in appreciation and the fire tongs did a little dance across the hearth.

Only the matches looked bored. "How easily amused you all are," they remarked with a yawn. "You know nothing of the world outside this place."

"I always tried to follow what was happening in the outside world," the cooking pot said mildly.

"The shopping basket brought home news from the marketplace each week, but things were always so busy here that it was hard to keep up with it all."

"What's the outside world got to do with us anyway?" said the knives and forks, who were rattled by the matches' comments.

"Enough of this bickering," bustled the broom. "It's time we got the house in order."

Just then, the door opened and in came the kitchen maid. The pots and pans froze on the spot.

"What a mess!" the maid exclaimed. "I'd better light a fire and clean up." She bent down and picked up the matches from the hearth.

"Now our time has come," they thought. "At last, everyone will see how we shine."

As the maid struck each one, it sputtered and burst into flame. But, after a brief moment of glory, the flame fizzled out.

The kitchen utensils watched solemnly as the matches' burned stubs were thrown into the grate. Silently, they each made a vow to be happy with what life had given them."

"And that's the end of the matches' story," finished the young man.

"What an amusing tale," the Sultan chuckled.

"But it has moral backbone too," the Sultana added thoughtfully.

"You liked my story?" asked the young man.

"Oh yes," said the Sultan and Sultana.

"Then may I have the princess's hand?" the young man beamed. Despite themselves, the Sultan and Sultana found themselves agreeing.

They even gave the young man a pouch of gold pieces to buy a wedding suit. But the merchant's son was still eager to impress his new family. So, instead, he used the gold to buy some fireworks.

The evening before the wedding, he loaded them into his trunk and flew up over the castle. There was a whistle and a crack as the first rocket burst, sending showers of stars cascading through the night sky. The Sultan and Sultana gaped in amazement at the flying trunk.

Soon, a large crowd had gathered. Every explosion lit up their upturned faces, and the young man could see their astonishment. He grinned with satisfaction at the spectacle he had created. "Now my time has come," he thought. "Everyone can see that I am *somebody*."

When the fireworks were over, he flew back to the forest to spend the last night before his wedding away from his bride.

As he lay down beside the trunk to sleep, he smiled contentedly. He didn't notice that a spark had settled inside it. While the young man slept, the spark glowed in the darkness.

Slowly and quietly it kindled a fire, and by the time he woke up the next morning, the trunk was burned to ashes.

The young man was absolutely distraught. How would he get to his princess in time for the wedding? In desperation, he set off on foot.

The princess waited for her beloved all day long, but he did not come. Eventually, as the sun was setting, the princess's angry parents gave orders for the castle gates to be locked.

When the young man arrived, he hammered
on the gates. "I'm sorry I missed the wedding.
I can explain," he called out.

The Sultan looked down from his window.
"How dare you show your face after what you've
done?" he stormed. "Who do you think you are?
We gave you a chance and this is how you
reward us. Now get out of here." And, with that,
the guards chased him away.

So that was the end of the young man's story.
He never did marry. Instead, he wandered the
world, telling his sad tale to anyone who would
listen. It was passed on from person to person,
until eventually it found its way here.

THE BRAVE TIN SOLDIER

The little boy opened his birthday present and nearly burst with excitement. Inside was a whole army of tin soldiers with matching red and blue uniforms and muskets over their shoulders.

He lined up the soldiers and they stood at attention. They all looked exactly the same, apart from one. This last soldier had only one leg because the toymaker had run out of tin when he was making him.

The little boy marched his new soldiers up and down. The one-legged soldier marched just as proudly as the rest, although he hobbled a little and found it hard to keep up.

As the others strode ahead, the soldier looked up at the boy's elaborate cardboard castle. It had tall turrets with pointed roofs, majestic ramparts and a grand gatehouse.

Standing on the castle was a pretty ballerina doll. She was cut out of paper and wore a delicate muslin dress with a sparkling tinsel sash around her waist.

But what struck the soldier most about her was that she had only one leg. "She's just like me," he thought. "I wonder if she'd agree to be my wife."

In fact, the ballerina had two legs, but one was just hidden behind the other, so the soldier couldn't see it from where he was standing. "I must speak to her," he decided.

So when the little boy marched the other soldiers back into their box, the one-legged soldier hid behind it and waited.

As soon as the little boy had gone to bed, a music box began to play and the toys came to life. The steam train chugged out of the station, the clockwork mice scurried across the floor and the rocking horse nodded in time to the music.

But the one-legged soldier only had eyes for

the ballerina doll. He watched in awe as she pirouetted along the castle ramparts. He had never seen anything so graceful.

The soldier sighed and shook his head. "It would never work," he murmured. "She lives in a castle and I live in a wooden box with twenty-four other soldiers. It's no place for a lady."

Just then, a jack-in-a-box burst out of his box. He leered at the soldier with a sinister grin. "Don't go getting ideas above your rank," he warned. "You never know what might happen."

The next morning, when the little boy came into the nursery, he found the one-legged soldier lying on the floor. He picked him up and placed him on the window ledge.

A moment later, a gust of wind caught the soldier, knocking him off balance. He wobbled dangerously and then toppled right out of the open window.

Head over heels the soldier tumbled, down and down and down. He landed in the street far below and lay there in a daze, too shocked to cry out for help. As he stared up at the sky, a raindrop splashed onto his face and then another and another.

The little boy came outside with the kitchen maid to look for the soldier, but as the rain grew heavier they gave up the search.

"The jack-in-a-box was right," thought the soldier helplessly. "A soldier should know his place. Now look what's happened to me."

Eventually, the rain stopped and two

newspaper delivery boys came splashing down the street. They found the poor soldier lying in a puddle. "He's all wet," said one, picking up the soldier and wiping him on his shirt.

"We should make him a boat," suggested the other. So they folded a piece of newspaper to make a boat. Then they tucked the soldier inside and sent him sailing down the gutter.

For a while the boys ran beside the boat, clapping and cheering, but the rushing water soon swept it away. "Goodbye, little soldier," they called after him.

The paper boat dipped and dived until the soldier felt seasick.

But he held on to his musket and stared bravely
ahead. Suddenly, the boat began to spin, and the
soldier found himself being sucked into a drain.
He clung on tightly as the boat swirled down into
the sewers below.

Now the soldier wasn't usually afraid of the
dark, but when he saw a pair of glinting eyes he
was rather alarmed. As he got closer, he saw that
it was a huge water rat. "Where do you think
you're going?" the rat demanded.

The soldier didn't answer.
He just gripped his musket
tighter and whirled past.

"Stop, intruder!" cried
the water rat.

At once, a pack of rats
rushed out of the tunnel

and chased after the flimsy boat, gnashing their teeth ferociously. The rats came closer and closer, until they were barely more than a whisker away.

Just in time, a glimmer of daylight appeared in the tunnel ahead. When the rats saw it, their pace slackened and the boat sped on.

The soldier shuddered at his narrow escape, but as the rush of water swelled to a roar his relief turned to horror. The boat was hurtling straight towards a waterfall.

Before the soldier had time to paddle back, a torrent of foamy water swept his boat over the edge. For a few moments, the soldier felt as though he and the boat were flying. Then they plunged into a canal.

At once, the boat filled up with water.

The sodden paper fell apart, tipping the soldier into the canal. He bobbed on the surface briefly. Then the waves closed over his head.

A picture of the pretty ballerina doll filled the soldier's mind as he sank deeper and deeper. "Will I ever see her again?" he thought miserably. "I'd give anything to be with her one last time."

Just when it seemed as though things couldn't possibly get any worse, the shadowy shape of an enormous fish loomed out of the deep.

"This really is the end," thought the unlucky soldier.

The fish's cavernous jaws gaped wide and closed around him, swallowing him whole.

Inside the belly of the fish, it was blacker than the darkest night. The soldier couldn't even see his musket ahead of him. He was trembling with fear and cold. But, as the fish swam through the water, the motion rocked him gently from side to side. Exhausted by his adventure, he found himself drifting into sleep.

The soldier was woken with a jolt as he slammed against the fish's ribs. It was thrashing around violently, hurling him this way and that. Then suddenly it was still.

For a long time, the soldier could hear nothing. Then came a gentle murmur of voices that gradually quietened down again.

At last, there was a flash like a lightning bolt.

Daylight cut through the darkness as the fish was sliced open. The soldier stared up and blinked at the bright light.

Peering down at him was the kitchen maid who had helped to look for him. Just by chance, she had been down to the fish market and bought the very fish that had eaten the soldier to cook for dinner. "Imagine that!" she chuckled.

The maid rinsed off the soldier and wiped him dry on her apron. Then she took him up to the nursery and set him down with the other soldiers.

As soon as she had left the room, the soldier's comrades crowded around him excitedly. "Welcome back," said the general, slapping him on the back. "It looks as though you've been on quite an adventure."

Filled with curiosity, the ballerina doll came

down from the castle to speak to the soldier herself. "Have you really been outside?" she asked.

The soldier nodded shyly and she gazed at him in wide-eyed admiration.

"I'd never be brave enough to do a thing like that," gasped the ballerina. "What's it like?"

The soldier was just about to tell her the story of his incredible adventures when the door burst open and the little boy ran in. "There you are," he cried.

The little boy inspected the tin soldier and

noticed that he was no longer shiny and new. Next to the others, he looked more out of place than ever. Without a second thought, the boy snatched him up and threw him into the fire.

As the flames licked around the brave tin soldier, he looked longingly at the ballerina doll. Bright sparks flew out of the fire like fireworks and he felt an intense warmth spread throughout his body. He wasn't sure whether it was the love he felt for her or the heat of the blaze.

"Don't go!" cried the ballerina, reaching out towards him. But, as she did, the flames caught hold of her, and she fluttered into the fire too.

For a moment, the tin soldier and the ballerina held one another in a fiery embrace, and they were happy. Then the blaze climbed higher and they disappeared from view.

By the time the maid came to sweep up the
ashes, the soldier and the ballerina doll were
nowhere to be seen. All that was left behind to
show that they had been there, was a little tin
heart, glowing in the embers.

THE WILD SWANS

Long ago in a faraway land, there lived a king with eleven sons and a single daughter whose name was Eliza. The children were happy and good, and very well cared for. They all loved one another very much.

Their mother had died years ago, and one day
the king decided to marry again. Unfortunately,
the queen he had chosen had an evil heart.

At the wedding, she gave the children sand
to eat instead of real food. They didn't dare
complain, but watched hungrily as all the other
guests feasted on cake and roasted apples.

After the wedding, the queen said sweetly
to the king, "Dear little Eliza needs to be sent
to a school for princesses. I know a lovely one
where all the best princesses go..."

"Good idea," said the king. "Let's send her
there right away."

But the queen had no intention of sending
Eliza to school. The very next day, she took her
to live with a poor woodcutter and his wife in
the woods.

She told them Eliza would cook and clean
for them. The woodcutter and his wife were so
in awe of the new queen, they didn't dare ask
why, but welcomed the princess into their home.
Eliza watched with sad eyes as the royal carriage
drove away without her.

The next day, the queen said to the king,
"My dear, your boys need to see the world to
finish their education. I have some friends in
exotic places. Shall I arrange something?"

The king was pleased she was taking such
an interest in the children. "Please do," he said.

So the queen summoned the eleven brothers
to the top of the highest tower and said:

"Leave this land and fly away.

Fly far away, fly far away,

like snow-white birds without a voice."

At once the eleven princes started to change.
Their bodies sprouted snow-white feathers.
Their necks grew long, and their mouths became
yellow beaks. They had turned into swans.
They opened their beaks to protest,
but no sound came out. So they
spread their wings and
flew up into the sky.

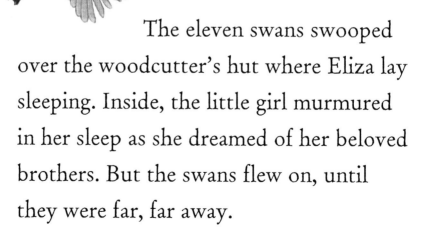

The eleven swans swooped
over the woodcutter's hut where Eliza lay
sleeping. Inside, the little girl murmured
in her sleep as she dreamed of her beloved
brothers. But the swans flew on, until
they were far, far away.

Years went by and Eliza grew
up, and the wind whispered to the roses
about how beautiful she was.

On her fifteenth birthday, a carriage arrived
at the woodcutter's hut. "The queen wants me to
bring the princess home," announced the driver.

"They must miss you at the palace," the
woodcutter's wife said to Eliza kindly. "We
certainly will here. Good luck, my dear."

Eliza kissed her on the cheek, and hugged
the woodcutter goodbye.

When she arrived at the palace, the queen was
waiting. "Your father has asked to see you," she
said looking the girl up and down. "You look
terrible. You'll need to take a bath first."

While the princess went into the bathroom, the queen paid a visit to the palace gardens and brought back three warty toads.

"Sit on her head so she turns as stupid as you," she said to the first.

"Sit on her forehead so she turns as ugly as you," she said to the second.

"Sit on her chest so her heart turns rotten," she said to the third.

The toads hopped away to do as they were told. But Eliza had such a good heart, that as soon as they touched her, they turned into harmless flowers floating in the bathwater.

Eliza came out of the bathroom looking lovelier than ever, and the queen seethed with anger. "I'll have to use stronger magic," she thought. To Eliza she said, in a voice as sweet as syrup, "Let me rub perfume into your skin."

She smeared a magic ointment on the girl's face and arms that made her look like a stranger, then showed her in to see the king.

Eliza's heart rose with happiness when she saw her father sitting on his throne. But the king didn't recognize her. "You're not my daughter," he said.

Poor Eliza turned away with tears in her eyes. "Be gone!" hissed the queen, and so she fled from the castle and into the deep forest.

She lost her way, and wandered through the trees, wondering what would become of her. When night fell, she lay down on the mossy ground. Fireflies gathered around her, and foxes stood guard as she slept.

In the morning, she came to a lake. She bathed in the water, and the magic ointment was washed away. Without even knowing what had happened, Eliza looked like herself again.

She found wild apples and berries for her breakfast, and the birds sang to her as she walked through the trees. She began to feel a little better as she went along. "But the only thing that would make me truly happy is finding my brothers," she said to herself.

Just then, she met a woman with bright green eyes. "Have you seen eleven princes pass this way?" asked Eliza.

"No," answered the woman, "but just this morning I saw eleven swans with gold crowns on their heads." And she showed Eliza the way to the river where she had seen them.

Eliza followed the river until it met the sea. On the shore, she found eleven snow-white feathers.

She picked them up and pressed them to her heart. "The sea has taken my brothers," she said, "and I'm sure the sea will bring them back." She waited patiently all day long, staring out at the endless waves.

Finally, when the sun was about to set, she spotted eleven tiny silhouettes in the sky. They flew closer and closer until she could see that they were swans with crowns on their heads.

As the last rosy rays of the sun streamed out over the water, the swans landed on the shore. Before Eliza's eyes, they began to change. They grew tall, and their feathers disappeared, and they became her eleven beloved brothers.

It had been years since her brothers had seen her, but they knew her right away. "Eliza!" they cried out, and she rushed into their open arms.

All night long they talked, telling one another everything that had happened. "Every morning at sunrise, we turn into swans," the eldest brother explained, "and we must fly away, far across the sea. Every sunset we become ourselves again."

"Eliza, will you come with us tomorrow?" asked the youngest brother. "I can't bear to leave you now we're together again."

"Of course I'll come," Eliza said.

They wove a hammock out of long sea grasses that grew on the shore. At sunrise, when her brothers turned into swans, Eliza climbed into the hammock, and they picked it up in their beaks and took flight.

All day long the eleven swans flew, their snow-white wings flashing against the sky. Eliza peered down through the clouds at the sapphire sea.

In the afternoon as the sun began to sink, she began to worry. There was no land in sight at all. When the sun began to drop below the horizon, she cried out in fear, "When you turn human we'll all fall into the sea and drown!"

Just as she spoke the swans began to dive. They dived quickly, as if they were falling, and Eliza gasped with fright.

Then she saw, far below them, waves foaming white around a small rock in the middle of the sea. Just as the last rays of the sun streamed out across the water, they all tumbled down onto the little rock, and the swans became princes again.

The rock was barely big enough to hold them all.

The brothers linked arms and stood around Eliza as the white waves foamed and crashed around them.

All night long the princes stood strong, until the sky paled into a yellow dawn, and they turned into swans once more.

They flew for another long day. This time, as Eliza peered down at the sea, she saw an island with bright flowers as big as cartwheels and a beautiful castle made of gold.

As she watched, the island was transformed into a fleet of golden ships with flower-bright sails. And then suddenly there was nothing there at all but curling mist.

They flew on and on until, at sunset, they reached another shore. "Did you see the fairy kingdom?" the youngest brother asked breathlessly as soon as he turned human.

Eliza nodded.

"It belongs to Fata Morgana, the fairy queen," her brother said. "We're lucky to have seen it."

They found a cave on the shore, made a fire and huddled around it for the night. As she drifted off to sleep, Eliza wished with all her heart to find a way to help her brothers.

In her dreams, Eliza saw the fairy queen. She had bright green eyes, and was very beautiful. She took Eliza by the hand. "I can tell you how to break the spell on your brothers..." she said, "but it will not be easy. You must pick stinging nettles with your bare hands, then make them into thread. From the thread you must weave eleven shirts for your eleven brothers. When you have finished all the shirts, your brothers must put them on, and the spell will be broken forever."

"Thank you!" cried Eliza.

"One more thing," said Fata Morgana. "Until the task is complete, you may not speak a single word. If you do, every one of your brothers will die on the spot."

When Eliza woke in the early light of dawn, she set to work immediately. She found a clump of nettles and picked them with her bare hands. They stung terribly and before long her hands were blistered and red.

Her brothers had already flown that morning, and when they came back in the evening and saw what she was doing they were aghast. "Is this some new enchantment?" asked the eldest.

Eliza could only shake her head and carry on.

"She can't speak," the youngest brother wept. "She's doing this to save us, I know it."

The whole night long Eliza worked, and at the end of it had made one shirt. The next day, her brothers flew away as swans again 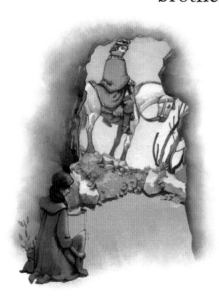 and she started work on the second shirt. Around midday, she heard galloping hooves, and a man on horseback appeared outside the cave.

"What are you doing here?" asked the rider.

Eliza could not say a word to explain herself.

"If you are as good as you are beautiful, you can come and rule my kingdom with me," said the king, for that was who he was.

When Eliza shook her head, the king thought she was just being shy. "Don't worry, I insist," he said. He lifted her onto his horse and took her back to his palace.

The king showed Eliza his city full of golden-domed buildings, she just stared blankly at it, and could think of nothing but the nettles and the shirts she'd left in the cave.

The king showed her his beautiful palace with its marble floors and wonderful paintings, and then he gave Eliza a pearl necklace and a ruby ring, but nothing could make her smile. And, of course, she couldn't speak a word.

"Perhaps she's a witch," said the king's advisor.

"Nonsense," answered the king. "Anyone who looks at this girl can tell how good she is."

He showed Eliza to her own room. "I hope you can be happy here," he said hopefully. His face fell when Eliza turned and looked wistfully out of the window.

Eliza knew that the king meant well, and she longed to be able to explain everything to him.

The next morning, the king came to her room. In his arms he held the bunch of nettles and the shirts Eliza had left in the cave.

"I don't understand what you were doing with these," he said, "but they seemed important to you..."

Eliza's face lit up. She seized the nettles and set to work on the third shirt right away.

The king watched her for a while, baffled, and then left her alone to carry on.

"She's clearly insane," said his advisor, when the king told him what had happened.

"She's nothing of the sort," the king retorted, although the girl's strangeness had begun to make him wonder.

By the evening, Eliza completed the third shirt, and had run out of nettles. "How can I get more?" she wondered. Out of the window, she could see into a graveyard, where clumps of nettles grew around the tombstones.

As it grew dark, Eliza hurried into the graveyard, and began collecting armfuls of nettles.

The king's advisor was watching. "She talks to the dead at night," he said to the king, and to anyone else who would listen.

The next day, Eliza wove another shirt, and the following night she went into the graveyard again to collect more nettles.

"She's gathering magic to destroy the city," the advisor declared.

By now, the king wasn't sure what to think.

Eliza continued to work every moment of every night and day. By the time she had finished the ninth shirt, the advisor had spread the word that a witch was plotting the city's ruin, and a crowd had gathered at the palace gates to demand that something be done.

Doubt had grown in the king's mind. "I don't think she's going to do any harm," he said uncertainly. "What do the people think?"

His advisor jumped at the chance to take charge. He rushed outside, and asked the crowd:

"Shall we allow the witch to destroy our city
or shall we save ourselves and burn her?"

"Burn her!" the people cried.

Poor Eliza was thrown into the dungeon,
clinging determinedly to her
nettles and shirts.

She worked all night long, while outside in
the market square, firewood was piled high.

As dawn paled outside the prison window,
Eliza began work on the final shirt.

Later, Eliza was taken to a cart and driven to the market square where the crowd was waiting. She barely noticed; she was weaving as fast as her blistered fingers could manage.

Then just as the cart drew to a halt, there came a whirring of wings, and eleven snow-white swans appeared in the sky. The crowd gasped at the sight.

The king had been watching in dismay, but when he saw the swans his heart surged with joy. "Stand back from the girl," he commanded. "Nobody evil could summon such pure birds."

The crowd drew back.

One by one, the swans landed on the cart beside Eliza, and she pulled a nettle shirt over each one's head. And as she did, the birds began to change.

Before the crowd's eyes, they grew tall and their feathers disappeared, and they became eleven princes with gold crowns on their heads.

But Eliza had not had time to finish the last shirt – it was missing a sleeve. Her youngest brother was the last in line, and when he transformed, he was left with one snow-white wing. He kept it for the rest of his life.

At last, Eliza was free to speak again, and so she told the crowd the whole story there and then. "So you see, I'm not a witch. I'm a princess," she ended.

Everyone was utterly ashamed to have believed the king's advisor. The king felt worst of all, and went down on his knees before Eliza. "Can you ever forgive me for not defending you?" he asked.

"You weren't to know," Eliza said kindly, and pulled him to his feet. But he went down on his knees once more, to ask for her hand in marriage.

Eliza married the king, and her eleven brothers were each given a portion of the kingdom to rule. They ruled wisely and well, and with great kindness. And, of course, they lived happily ever after.

As for the advisor, he was banished to a faraway land, and never seen again. Word had it that he told his story to an evil queen, who turned him into a warty toad... but perhaps that's just a fairy tale.

THE LITTLE FIR TREE

In the dappled shade of a forest glade a tiny fir tree grew. The little tree longed to grow up, and each morning it would stretch up its branches towards the sun's rays as they shone down through the trees.

One day, as the fir tree listened to the birds singing in the treetops, it gave a sigh. "If only I were as strong and tall as those trees," it said. "Then the birds would nest among my branches and all the young trees would look up to me."

The old pine tree shook its gnarled head. "You shouldn't wish your youth away," it warned. "There will come a time when you'd be glad of what you have now."

But the fir tree paid no attention. It was fed up with being rooted to the spot with the same old view, day after day. It couldn't wait to extend its head above the forest and see the big wide world beyond.

That afternoon, some children came into the forest to collect berries. "What a pretty little tree," they said when they saw the fir tree.

The fir tree's needles
bristled with indignation
and it pulled itself up,
trying to look taller. But
the children were too
busy munching their
berries to notice.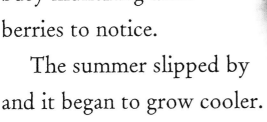

The summer slipped by
and it began to grow cooler.
Soon, woodcutters arrived with their
axes slung over their shoulders. The fir tree
watched curiously as they hacked at the trunk
of the old pine tree.

As the tree fell to the ground, it gave a hollow
moan. The fir tree shuddered. In its short life, it
had never heard a tree make such a sound before.

The fir tree looked on in wonder as several

more of the tallest trees were cut down and loaded onto the waiting carts.

Without the shelter of its taller companions, the fir tree soon felt winter's frosty nip. The clouds grew heavy and snowflakes drifted down from the sky. As they settled on the fir tree's branches, it shivered with cold, sprinkling a nearby hare with snow.

"Watch out!" cried the hare, and it hopped over the fir tree and bounded on its way.

The fir tree stared after it crossly. It didn't like to be reminded of its lack of height.

The winter was long and harsh, but eventually the snow melted and the first signs of spring appeared. Streams hurried over the rocks, armies of caterpillars marched up the trees and the swallows returned from their long migration. "Where have all the big trees gone?" they asked.

"The woodcutters took them away," replied the fir tree. "I don't know where they've taken them. Didn't you see them on your travels?"

At first, the swallows shook their heads. Then one of them remembered something it had seen. "Out at sea, there was a fleet of tall ships," it said slowly. "I'm sure the trees were standing on the decks. They were holding up the sails and looked so stately and proud."

"That sounds like a wonderful life," said the fir tree enviously. "What's the sea like?"

"It's so vast that I flew for weeks and still didn't reach the end of it," said the swallow.

"Oh how I wish I were big enough to sail on the sea," said the fir tree.

The fir tree grew more and more distant from the life of the forest, shrugging off the sweet morning dew, batting away the butterflies and ignoring the ants that tickled his roots. It didn't even take any notice when the sparrows began to nest among its branches. All it could think about was a life on the ocean waves.

Gradually, the sun grew cooler; the nights grew longer and the days became shorter. The woodcutters returned, and this time they began to fell some of the smaller, more beautiful trees.

"Those trees aren't tall enough to be ships' masts," muttered the fir tree as the woodcutters took them away. "Where can they be going?"

"We know! We know!" chirped the sparrows. "They're taking them to the town over the hill. We've seen trees just like them through the windows, all dressed up. You should see how they glitter and sparkle."

"Perhaps one day that will be my fate too," said the fir tree longingly. "I don't see what they have that I don't."

"A few more rings in their trunks," butted in the hare mischievously. Then, much to the fir tree's annoyance, the little creature leaped right over it once again.

Throughout the winter, the fir tree felt a warm glow in spite of the cold. It had forgotten all about its dreams of ocean adventure. Instead, the tree imagined itself in a snug house adorned with pretty decorations, with people all gathered around to admire it.

Eventually, the tap, tap, tap of the woodpecker's beak sounded the arrival of spring and jolted the fir tree from its daydreams.

By the time summer came, the fir tree's trunk had grown fatter and its branches had become thicker and darker green. It held its head higher too.

In fact, the fir tree had grown so tall that when the hare next came by, it had to run around it.

That winter, the woodcutters came back to the forest. This time, one of them stopped right beside the fir tree. "What a handsome tree!" he exclaimed. "I don't think I need to search any further." The fir tree swelled with pride. At last, its time had come.

The woodcutter's axe bit into its trunk, and the fir tree let out a gasp. It swayed to and fro and then crashed to the ground.

As the woodcutters heaved the fir tree onto a cart, it gazed up at the trees and its familiar patch of sky. Suddenly, it felt limp with sadness, for it knew then that it would never see the forest again.

The bumpy journey to the town passed by in a blur, and the fir tree only started to feel better as it was carried into a snug living room and placed upright again.

Being inside a house was even more impressive than he had imagined. Patterns covered the walls all around him, a warm fire flickered in an elegant fireplace, and a pretty, glowing light hung from the ceiling.

Everything seemed to happen very quickly after that. The tree's branches were decorated with baubles and candles, tinsel garlands were draped around its trunk and brightly wrapped presents with silk bows were stacked beneath it.

"If only the hare could see me now," thought the fir tree as a gold star was placed on top.

By the time the candles were lit the tree was so excited that it began to tremble and one of its branches caught fire. Hastily, the servants put out the flames. They were just in time. For, at that moment, the master and mistress of the house came in with their young children.

When the children saw how magical the fir tree looked, their faces lit up. As they rushed over to the tree, they almost knocked it down in their enthusiasm. There were shouts of delight as they unwrapped their presents and discovered dainty porcelain dolls, smart tin soldiers and a shiny train set.

Once all the presents were opened, the children sat down near the fire and begged their father to tell them a story.

The fir tree listened, entranced, as he told the story of Humpty Dumpty and how he fell off a wall, but recovered and married a princess.

"Another one, another one," the children cried when the story was finished.

But by now the fir tree's candles had burned down. "Tomorrow," promised their father, and the children went reluctantly to bed.

After they had gone, the fir tree stared contentedly into the embers of the fire, wondering what the next day would bring.

But, when morning came, the children were far too busy playing with their new toys to pay the fir tree any attention.

Eventually, the servants came and hauled the fir tree away to a cold, dark woodshed, with cobwebs hanging from the ceiling. The fir tree couldn't understand why it had been left there.

"There must be some mistake," the fir tree reasoned. "I'm sure they'll come back and get me soon. Perhaps they'll plant me out in the garden when it gets a little warmer."

But days and weeks went by and no one came. The fir tree grew more and more lonely.

It thought fondly of the forest and often wished that it was back there.

One evening, the fir tree's thoughts were interrupted by a scuffling noise. It looked down and saw three little mice scurry across the floor.

They stopped when they saw the tree and looked up inquisitively. "Who are you?" "Where do you come from?" "What are you doing here?" they squeaked in turn.

"One question at a time," chuckled the fir tree, happy to have some company. It told them all about the forest where it had grown up and the birds that sang in the trees. It described the warm, breezy summers and long, snowy winters.

The mice listened eagerly, for they had never heard about such things. "It sounds wonderful," they said. "You must have been so happy."

"I suppose I was," said the fir tree
wistfully, "but I always wanted to see
more of the world."

Then it told them all about
Christmas in the grand living room.
The fir tree described the glittering
decorations, the children's glee
when they opened their presents
and how it had heard the story
of Humpty Dumpty.

"Please tell us the story,
old fir tree," begged the
little mice.

"Less of the old," mumbled the fir tree, pretending to be cross, but it told them the story all the same.

The next night, the mice brought some of their friends to hear the story of Humpty Dumpty. Delighted to have such an appreciative audience, the fir tree told the story once again.

"Tell us another," they pleaded when the story was finished.

"I'm afraid I don't know any more," said the fir tree in a slightly crestfallen voice.

"What a pity," said the mice, and they all scampered off.

The fir tree waited and waited, but the mice didn't return to the woodshed the next night, or any of the nights after that, and the fir tree felt lonelier than ever.

At last, one morning, the door of the woodshed opened, and the servants dragged the fir tree out into the garden. "Now life is beginning again," it thought.

The tree stretched out its branches to soak up the sunshine, but as it did so, the last of its needles fell off, leaving its branches bare.

Just then, the children came out to play. When the youngest one saw the fir tree, she skipped towards it. For a moment the tree's heart leapt, but she just snatched the gold star from the top.

"Look what I found on the bare old fir tree," she cried, chasing after the others.

The fir tree looked around at the pretty flowers in the garden. Then it stared down at itself. When it saw how bedraggled it had become, the fir tree felt ashamed and wished that it was back in the woodshed out of sight.

Meanwhile, the servants were piling up twigs and branches in the corner of the garden.

"That's strange," thought the fir tree as they set them alight. "Why are they making a fire when it's already so warm?"

But before the fir tree had time to think of an explanation, the servants grabbed it and threw it on top of the fire.

As the flames licked around it, the fir tree was reminded of that happy Christmas in front of the roaring fire. Then it thought back to its time in the forest and imagined the warm summer sun shining down.

The fir tree sighed. "I didn't realize at the time, but they were truly happy days. I had the loveliest friends, and a beautiful place to live. If only I had enjoyed it while I could."

But that was all in the past, and now the fir tree's own story had come to an end too.

THE TINDERBOX

Left, right, left, right! A lone soldier came marching up the road, his eyes fixed on the horizon. At last, he could see the rooftops of the city.

"Good evening, Soldier," came a husky voice from behind him.

The soldier turned around to see a stooped old woman. "Good evening, Madam," he said, taking off his cap to her.

"What's the news from the battlefront?" croaked the old woman.

"The war is over," the soldier told her cheerfully. "So I'm off to the city to make my fortune and to find myself a wife."

The old crone grinned. "Perhaps you and I could help each other out," she said.

"Really?" asked the soldier. "How?"

"You see that tree with the hole in its trunk?" she said, pointing a bony finger at a gnarled old tree. "If you climb down inside it you'll find three chests full of money."

The soldier eyed the old woman suspiciously. "And what do you want in return?" he asked.

"All I want is for you to find my old tinderbox that I have lost down there," she replied.

"That sounds easy enough," said the soldier. "It's a deal." And he started to climb into the tree.

"Wait," said the crone. "It isn't all that easy. You'll have to get past three fierce-looking guard dogs. One has eyes the size of saucers, the second has eyes as big as dinner plates and the third has eyes as wide as cartwheels. But don't worry. Take my blue apron and lay it on the ground. Get each dog onto the apron and it will lie down as docile as a kitten."

She handed the soldier her apron and the end of a length of rope. "However, the dogs won't stay still for long," she warned him. "Tie this rope around your waist and I'll pull you up as soon as you're ready to come out."

"Thanks," said the soldier, and with the rope around his waist, he climbed into the tree and lowered himself down inside. At the bottom, he untied himself and peered around.

He was in a gloomy cavern. Three chambers opened off the cavern, and out of each one stared a pair of glinting eyes.

The soldier spread out the old woman's blue apron on the ground, then went into the first chamber. There, guarding a wooden chest full of copper coins, was a huge, ferocious-looking guard dog.

Just as the crone had described, the dog's eyes were the size of saucers. They bulged out of its head as it stared threateningly at the soldier.

"Didn't anyone tell you it's rude to stare?" joked the soldier. Then he grabbed the dog by the scruff of its neck. It snarled and snapped as the soldier dragged it out into the cavern, but as soon as he hauled it onto the old woman's apron, it whimpered, lay down and fell asleep.

"Well, that was easy enough!" said the soldier. He poured the copper coins into his backpack and moved on to the second chamber.

There, the second dog was guarding a chest full of silver coins. It was bigger and more monstrous than the last, and its eyes were the size of dinner plates. With its unblinking eyes fixed on the soldier, the dog let out a deep, rumbling growl and bared its dagger-sharp teeth.

"Don't you look at me like that," said the soldier and he grabbed the dog and heaved it over to the old woman's apron. Just as before, the dog instantly lay down and fell asleep with its head between its paws. The soldier scooped all the silver coins into his bag and hurried on.

In the third chamber was a chest full of gold coins. But blocking the way was the biggest, most terrifying dog yet. It towered over the soldier, and it had impossibly big eyes – eyes as wide as cartwheels.

The dog let out a blood-curdling howl, then something really extraordinary happened. Its eyes began to spin around and around in their sockets, faster and faster. The soldier stared in amazement until he was dizzy.

Slavering murderously, the dog roared and made a dive for the soldier. At the very last moment, the soldier ducked. The dog flew right over him, knocking off his hat and landing on the apron with a ground-shuddering thud.

Just like the others, the dog instantly slumped down on the apron and began to snooze.

"What dozy dogs!" exclaimed the soldier. Quickly, he crammed all the gold coins into his bag. "With all this money, I'll be able to buy anything I want!" he thought.

The first dog was beginning to stir when the soldier spotted the old woman's tinderbox at the bottom of the chest. He reached in and grabbed it, then ran to the rope.

"Madam, please pull me up as quick as you can," he called, tugging on the rope.

The rope didn't move. "Have you found my tinderbox?" came the old woman's voice.

Suddenly all three dogs shook the sleep from their eyes and sprang to their feet, snarling. "Yes, yes, I've got it," called the soldier. "Now please pull me up before the dogs get me!"

"Very well," she said.

The dogs leaped up and down trying to sink their teeth into the soldier's ankles, but the woman hoisted him up to safety, just in the nick of time.

The soldier climbed out of the hole in the tree trunk and breathed a sigh of relief.

"That was close," he said. "A moment longer and those vicious dogs would have torn me limb from limb."

"Yes, and they still will!" cackled the old woman. She snatched the tinderbox from the soldier, then tried to push him back into the tree.

But the soldier pushed back, knocking the tinderbox from the old woman's hand. She lunged forward to pick it up, tripped over one of the tree's twisted roots and went tumbling down the hole.

The soldier shuddered. "I wonder why the old woman was so desperate to get hold of this battered thing," he thought as he picked up the tinderbox and turned it over in his hands. "It looks perfectly ordinary to me, but it might come in useful."

So he put the tinderbox in his backpack, along with the copper, silver and gold coins, and headed off to the city.

When he arrived, he went straight to the best hotel in town, booked himself into its most luxurious set of rooms and ordered every dish on the menu to be sent up to him.

The next day, the soldier went on a shopping spree. He bought himself a stylish winter coat with big, brass buttons, some shiny black leather boots and a dappled silver mare to ride around town.

Over the next few weeks, the soldier made many new friends. They told him all the wonderful things there were to see and do in their city, and showed him the copper castle up on the hill.

"Who lives there?" the soldier asked.

"The king, queen and their daughter," his friends replied. "The princess is said to be incredibly beautiful, but we've never seen her. A fortune teller once said that she was destined to marry an ordinary soldier. The king doesn't ever want that to happen, so he keeps her locked away in the castle."

"I must find a way to see her," thought the soldier. "Perhaps I'm the soldier she's supposed to marry."

Over the next few weeks, he led a merry life. He passed the days riding in the royal parks, spent evenings at the opera, and danced the nights away at balls and parties. Then one day, he suddenly found that he had just two gold coins left.

The soldier had to move out of his luxurious rooms, and into a cheap attic space. He sold his coat and his horse, and got himself a job washing dishes to pay the rent.

It was dark in the attic, but the soldier didn't even have a spare penny to buy a candle. Then, one evening, he remembered that he still had the old woman's tinderbox.

Opening up the box, he found a flint and the stub of a candle. He took them out and struck the flint against the side of the box. No sooner had it sparked, than the guard dog with eyes as big as saucers appeared. It was wagging its tail and didn't look so fierce any more.

"What may I do for you, Master?" asked the dog.

The soldier was astounded. "Well, this is a welcome surprise!" he exclaimed. "I really need some money. I don't suppose you could bring me some could you?"

"Your wish is my command," answered the dog. In the blink of a saucer-sized eye, it vanished and reappeared with a sack of copper coins in its mouth.

"Good dog," said the soldier, and he patted the creature on the head.

The next evening, he took out the tinderbox again to light another candle. He struck the flint against the side of the box and in a flash the dog with eyes the size of dinner plates appeared, wagging its tail and ready to obey his wishes.

The soldier soon learned that whenever he needed money, he could simply strike the tinderbox to summon one of the guard dogs to bring him another sack of copper, silver or gold coins.

The soldier gave up his dishwashing job and returned to a life of leisure. He moved into a large townhouse, bought back his silver mare, and ate out every night. Every morning, he went riding in the royal park and looked up at the high walls that surrounded the copper castle. He longed to see the beautiful princess who was locked up inside.

Then, one evening, the soldier had idea. He struck the tinderbox and in a flash the dog with the eyes the size of saucers appeared. "What may I do for you, Master?" it asked.

"It's nearly midnight, but I'd love just a brief glimpse of the princess," said the soldier.

"Your wish is my command," replied the dog. It turned tail and vanished, returning a moment later with the very sleepy princess riding on its back.

She had tumbling coppery curls and her nightdress was embroidered with silver and gold stars. The soldier thought she was the most beautiful woman he had ever seen. He couldn't resist giving her a quick kiss on the cheek before the dog whisked her back to the castle.

The next morning, the princess ate breakfast with the king and queen. "I had the strangest dream last night," she told them. "I dreamed that a dog with eyes as big as saucers came to my room, and I rode on its back across the rooftops to where a handsome soldier was waiting for me – and he kissed me."

The king scowled. "What an unlikely tale!" he said. But he was secretly worried that it wasn't a dream at all. So, later, he ordered a maid to keep watch by the princess's bed and find out what was going on.

All day, the soldier could think of nothing but the beautiful princess. "I have to see her again," he sighed. So that night, he struck the tinderbox once more. In a flash, the dog with eyes the size of dinner plates appeared. "What may I do for you, Master?" it asked.

"I just want another brief glimpse of the beautiful princess," said the soldier.

"Your wish is my command," replied the dog, and it was gone. In no time at all, the dog returned with the sleeping princess on its back, just as before.

But this time, the princess's maid had been keeping watch. She followed the dog and watched it take her mistress into the soldier's house. She took a piece of chalk and marked the door with an 'x'. "Now I'll be able to find this place in the morning," she thought, and she went home to bed.

Soon after, the dog took the sleeping princess back to the castle. Being a clever dog, it noticed the cross on its master's front door. So it took a piece of chalk in its mouth and drew an 'x' on the door of every house in the city.

Early the next morning, the maid returned with the king and queen to show them where the dog had taken the princess. "Here it is," she announced, when they came to a house with a marked front door.

"No, there it is!" said the king, pointing to the front door of a house on the other side of the road. It had an 'x' on it too.

At the same moment, the queen called from the opposite side of the street, "Here it is!"

Realizing they had been outwitted, they went back to the castle to come up with another plan.

That night, the soldier struck the tinderbox again. This time, the dog with eyes as wide as cartwheels appeared. "What may I do for you, Master?" it asked.

Again, the soldier said he all he wanted was to see the beautiful princess.

"Your wish is my command," replied the dog and off it went. It carried the sleeping princess on its back over the rooftops, through the streets of the sleeping city and to the soldier's house.

In spite of its enormous eyes, there was something the dog hadn't noticed. Earlier that day, the queen had sewn a pouch full of flour to the back of the princess's nightdress. Then, she cut a small hole in it. All the way from the castle, the flour had trickled out, leaving a trail that led straight to the soldier's house.

At dawn, the soldier was woken by the noise of someone pounding at his front door. Throwing on his dressing gown, he opened the door to be confronted by the king and his officers.

"Seize him!" cried the king. The soldier was marched to the city prison and thrown in a dark, damp cell. "You'll hang this afternoon!" bellowed the king.

Alone in his cell, the soldier stared through the bars of the tiny window. Outside, the king's officers were building a gallows in the market square, and a crowd was already gathering to watch the hanging. "How am I going to get out of this?" he wondered.

Then, he had an idea. He called out to a boy in the street, "Hey, Boy. If you go to my house and bring me my tinderbox from the kitchen dresser, I'll give you a gold coin."

The boy had never been offered so much as a copper penny before, so he agreed to help. Before long, he returned with the tinderbox.

No sooner had the soldier paid the boy, than two of the king's officers unlocked the door of the cell. They led the him out to the square, where the whole city was now waiting. The king and queen were sitting on a splendid throne, and it seemed the only person who was missing was the princess.

As the hangman took him up the steps to the gallows, the soldier spoke up. "May I have a last request?" he asked. "I'd dearly like to smoke my pipe once more, before I die."

"Very well!" said the king.

The soldier reached into his pocket and pulled out a pipe and the tinderbox. Once, twice, three times he struck the flint against the box. In a flash, all three dogs appeared. The crowd gasped, and the hangman fainted.

"What may we do for you, Master?" the dogs asked all together.

"Please bring the princess here to me," said the soldier.

"Your wish is our command, Master," replied the dogs, and they vanished, leaving the king and queen wide-eyed in amazement.

In the blink of an eye, the dogs reappeared, bringing the princess with them. She beamed with delight as soon as she set eyes on the soldier. "My soldier!" she cried. "I knew you weren't just a dream."

"My princess!" the soldier replied. Then he turned to the king and queen. "Your daughter shouldn't be locked away. She should be free to marry any man she chooses," he said. "But I hope that man will be me."

The king felt suddenly ashamed. "You're right," he said. "You may be an ordinary soldier, but you are clearly extraordinarily brave to be able to command such terrifying creatures. I'd be happy to have you as a son-in-law as long as my daughter will have you."

"I will!" the princess replied happily.

And so, the princess married her soldier. The wedding feast was a grand affair, and the three dogs were all invited. They sat at the top table with the bride and groom, and watched over the party with their eyes as big as saucers, dinner plates and cartwheels.

THE Snow Queen

I

Little Kay and Gerda were the best of friends. They lived next door to one another, in two houses so close that from their bedroom windows they could almost join hands.

Between their bedroom windows was a tiny roof garden full of roses, where Gerda and Kay would play together all summer long.

In the winter, they huddled up in Gerda's warm kitchen, and listened to her grandmother's stories. One evening, she told them about the Snow Queen. "On a winter's night, she breathes frost on the windows," she said. The children had seen frost on the windows, and so they knew the Snow Queen must be real. "If the Snow Queen had her way, she'd turn everything to ice, including your heart," Grandmother warned.

"Just let her try!" said Kay bravely, shivering at the thought.

"Don't worry," Grandmother reassured him. "She can't conquer your heart unless you let her."

That night when Kay went home, the first snow of winter began to fall. He sat on his bed and gazed out at the silent, swirling snowflakes. All at once, a lady appeared. She looked icy and beautiful, and she peered through the window at Kay with glittering eyes.

"The Snow Queen," Kay gasped. In a rush of excitement, he opened the window. The Snow Queen reached out with one long finger and stroked his cheek. An icy chill ran down little Kay's spine. Then, in a dazzling whirl of snowflakes, she vanished into thin air.

Kay never told Gerda that he had seen the Snow Queen. In fact, after a while he began to wonder whether it had just been a dream. The winter passed, and he gradually forgot all about it. Summer came and the roses bloomed, and he and Gerda played together in their little roof garden.

But Kay wasn't the boy he used to be. He didn't feel right in the summer sunshine, and longed for winter again. The cold feeling in him grew and grew. One day, when they were watering the roses together, Kay cried out in pain. "My eye!" he wailed, clasping his hands over his eye, and, "My chest! Oh, it hurts!"

"Poor Kay, what's wrong?" asked Gerda anxiously. She looked into his eye and at his chest, but couldn't see anything there.

In truth, when Kay had opened the window to see the Snow Queen, a tiny fragment of ice from her breath had become stuck in his eye, and another had stuck in his heart. Gradually their power had grown and grown. Now, the splinter in his eye spoiled everything he saw, and the splinter in his heart turned it icy cold.

"This is a stupid game," he said crossly, kicking over the watering can.

"Let's go and ask my grandmother to tell us a story," Gerda suggested.

"That's boring!" said Kay. "I don't want to play with you any more. I'm going to play in the square with the other boys."

Gerda was so upset she couldn't think what to say. She just stood and watched Kay leave. This wasn't the boy she knew.

The summer days cooled, and winter came. Nothing pleased Kay the way it used to. He was restless and rude, and deeply unhappy.

One day, he was playing with the other boys in the town square when a large, white sleigh appeared. Inside was the Snow Queen. She smiled at the little boy, and her eyes glittered like ice. Kay was utterly enchanted.

He ran alongside the sleigh until it slowed down, and the Snow Queen leaned out and beckoned to him. "Come with me," she said.

Kay climbed eagerly into the sleigh. The Snow Queen wrapped him in her long, soft cloak, and it was like sinking into a snowdrift. Then she kissed his forehead, and his skin turned icy cold. She kissed him again and he went numb all over, and forgot about everything but her.

The sleigh drove out of the town in a whirl of snowflakes. The boys in the square carried on with their games. It was as if they had hardly noticed the strange sleigh at all.

When Kay didn't come home, little Gerda asked the boys if they had seen him. They shrugged their shoulders and couldn't remember. "Oh dear," said Gerda. "He often played with his sleigh on the frozen river. I hope he didn't fall into the water and drown..."

In the weeks that followed, Gerda and her grandmother wept for poor lost Kay.

II

Spring arrived with still no sign of Kay. Gerda looked out of her bedroom window at his empty one and missed him terribly.

Everybody believed Kay must have fallen through the ice on the river and drowned. But somehow, in her heart of hearts, Gerda didn't really believe that he was dead. So, when the twittering swallows returned, she put on her new red shoes and walked down to the river.

"If I give you the thing I love best," she said to the river, "will you give me back my Kay?"

She threw the shoes in, but the river washed them back to her. "Are you telling me you don't have Kay?" Gerda asked. "Or didn't I throw my shoes far enough?"

She climbed into a little boat on the shore, rowed out and dropped her shoes in the water again. All at once the river took the boat and swept it downstream. "Are you taking me to Kay?" asked Gerda.

The river didn't answer. It carried Gerda far, far downstream, through grassy meadows, along wooded banks, and further than she had ever been before.

They came to a bend in the river, with a pretty garden full of flowers in front of a small thatched cottage. The boat drew into shore.

Just then, an old lady came out of the cottage. She was wearing a flowery sunhat and smiled sweetly at Gerda. "Come inside," she said.

Inside the cottage, there was a bowl of ripe cherries on the table. "Help yourself," the old lady said, "and tell me what brings you here."

Gerda ate the sweet cherries and told the old lady everything, from the roses on the rooftop, to her search for little Kay. As Gerda talked, the old lady brushed her hair.

The more cherries Gerda ate, and the more the old lady brushed her hair, the more distant Kay seemed to become, and in the end, Gerda forgot all about him. In fact, she forgot why she was there at all.

The old lady had cast a spell on Gerda to make her forget everything. She didn't mean Gerda any harm. She was lonely, and just wanted the pretty little girl to stay and keep her company. "Come outside and see my garden," she said.

She led Gerda into the garden. Every imaginable flower was growing there. There were sunflowers, daisies, honeysuckle and marigolds, foxgloves, freesias, lavender... and roses.

While Gerda was admiring the daisies, the old lady hurried over to the roses. "Hide yourselves!" she hissed. "You'll only remind the girl of her friend, and make her want to leave me."

She tapped the rosebush with her walking stick and it sank beneath the ground.

For many days, Gerda stayed at the old lady's house, eating cherries and playing in the garden without a thought in the world for Kay.

One day, the old lady put on her flowery sunhat, and Gerda suddenly noticed a flower on it that she hadn't seen in the garden. It was a rose.

She wandered out into the garden thinking to herself, "Where have I seen this lovely flower before? It reminds me of something…"

Then, all at once, everything flooded back to her – she remembered her home, the rooftop with the roses, and her dear playmate Kay.

"What am I doing here when I should be looking for Kay?" she gasped.

Tears fell from her eyes and dropped on to
the ground just where the rosebush lay buried.
It sprang out of the soil.

"I need to find Kay," Gerda blurted at it.
"I don't know if he's dead but I need to try."

To her surprise, the roses whispered back.
"We've been underground; he is not buried
there," they said. "That means he is not dead.
Go and find him. Hurry before the old lady
stops you."

So Gerda rushed out of the garden without
even saying goodbye.

III

The summer had gone, and a cold wind blew the leaves from the trees. Gerda hurried along, wondering where to look for Kay, when she met a glossy black crow.

"Krah, krah," said the crow.

"Good day to you, Sir," Gerda answered politely.

To her surprise, the crow spoke. "Apparently you do not speak Crow, so I will try to speak your language," he said. "Where are you going, so alone in the world?"

So Gerda told the crow her whole story, from the roses on the rooftop to her search for little Kay, and how she'd spent too long in the old lady's garden and must hurry and find him.

The crow cocked his head. "Humans look all the same to me, but I might have seen your friend... My sweetheart, who is a crow like me, lives in a palace. She told me that the princess there wanted a husband. All the princes she met were handsome but empty-headed. But then a boy came from far away. He had squeaky boots but he was clever and bright, and the princess was very pleased with him. Now he lives at the palace with her."

"Oh, that could be Kay!" Gerda cried out in delight. "His boots did squeak and he is clever and bright. Please can you show me the palace?"

The crow led the way through a forest to a fine palace, surrounded by a high wall.

"Krah, krah!" called the crow, and another crow flew out from the palace garden to greet them. The crows talked together first in their own language, and then turned to Gerda.

"You will not be allowed through the palace gates without shoes," said the palace crow. "Only humans with shoes may go in. But I can take you to see this boy."

She showed Gerda through a gap in the garden wall, and they hid among the perfumed flowers. It was evening already, and the palace windows were full of golden lights. They waited in the dark until eventually the lights went out one by one. Then the crow said, "Follow me."

They crept into the palace through the door to the kitchens. They padded up the dark stairs, and out onto a corridor covered in deep rugs, which were warm and soft beneath Gerda's bare toes.

The crow led Gerda through a carved wooden door into a bedroom, with two beds shaped like large flowers. In one lay a sleeping princess, and in the other lay a boy, his face hidden by his arm.

Eagerly, Gerda put her hand on the boy's shoulder. "Kay, wake up. It's me, Gerda," she whispered.

The boy jumped as he woke up, and stared at Gerda in surprise. "Who are you?" he said.

Gerda let out a little cry. The boy wasn't Kay after all. She had never seen him before in her life. "I'm sorry. I thought you were someone else," she said miserably.

The princess in the next bed had woken up too. She said, "What brings you here? Perhaps we can help you."

So Gerda told them everything, from the
roses on the rooftop to her search for little Kay,
and how the two crows had tried to help her.

The princess looked at the palace crow, which
was standing near her bed. "As a reward for
helping this little girl," she told her, "you and
the other crow may eat all you like from my
kitchen for the rest of your lives."

"Krah!" said the crow, looking very pleased.

The princess turned to Gerda. "In the
morning we will send you on your way with
a carriage and horses, and a coachman to drive
them. That should make your search easier."

Gerda couldn't thank her enough.

So in the morning, after a filling breakfast,
she was sent on her way in a golden carriage,
with new shoes and a warm cloak.

The princess and the boy waved goodbye, and the crows flew after the carriage a little way. Then the carriage entered a thick wood and they were lost from view.

IV

The golden carriage glinted and glimmered through the dark trees. It hadn't gone very far when a group of robbers appeared on horseback. "This carriage is ours now!" the leader shouted. "Let's kill the driver." The terrified coachman fled, leaving Gerda all alone with the robbers.

"What shall we do with this little girl?" asked the leader, peering in through the window.

A dark-eyed robber girl looked in too. "I'll keep her as a pet," she said. She opened the door and pulled Gerda out. She took Gerda's new cloak and shoes to wear herself, and sat the girl on the back of her horse.

Together the robbers rode back to their lair, which was a ruined house in the thickest, most forgotten part of the woods.

The robber girl showed Gerda the room where she slept. Then she went over to a stall in the corner of the room and led a sorry-looking reindeer out by a rope around its neck.

"This is Ba," she said. "I keep him tied up or he'd run away."

The robber girl looked darkly at Gerda, and pulled out a glinting knife from her belt. "Don't you try to run away or I'll kill you," she said.

Then she grinned. "Now tell me a story. Make it a good one, or I might kill you anyway."

"Well," said Gerda, "I'm not sure if this is a good story... but it's certainly a true one." Then she told the robber girl her own story, from the roses on the rooftop at home to her search for little Kay, and how the crows and the princess and boy had tried to help her.

"Coo, coo," said a pigeon from the rafters. "I have seen this Kay of yours. He was riding in a sleigh with the Snow Queen. I don't know where they were going."

The reindeer spoke up in a low, velvet voice. "I know where they'd go," he said. "The Snow Queen lives in snowy Lapland, where I'm from."

The robber girl said, "Silence, all of you!" and they all jumped with fright. She frowned and looked at Gerda a moment. "It *was* a good story. All my animals seem to want to help you, so I suppose I ought to help you too," she said. She untied the reindeer, "Do you know how to get to Lapland, Ba?" she asked.

The reindeer looked at her with his dark, liquid eyes, and nodded solemnly.

"Then take this girl there to find her playmate," said the robber girl. "Do it quickly before I change my mind."

She helped Gerda onto the reindeer's back, and pushed a loaf of bread into her hand.

"I hope you find him," she said gruffly.

"Thank you," said Gerda, and the reindeer leaped into the night, and they were away.

Ba ran like the wind, through the forest and out onto the plains under a starry sky, further

and further north all the time. Wolves howled and owls hooted, and the air hissed with cold. Strange emerald and blue lights flashed across the sky above them. "They're the Northern Lights," said the reindeer. "That means we're nearly there."

The air grew so cold it felt as if it might crack, and soon all they could see around them was sparkling snow. They shared the loaf, and carried on and on through the snow, until Gerda's hands were frozen into the reindeer's coat, and her whole body was numb with cold.

At last they came to a small hut. The reindeer stopped, and tapped at the door with his hoof. A small, bent woman let them inside. She gave the little girl some warm soup, and while she was drinking it, Ba told their story.

"I know you are very clever," said the
reindeer in his soft, velvet voice. "You can tie
all the winds together, and loosen them one
at a time to blow a snowdrift this way or that.
Won't you help this little girl?"

"How would I help her?" said the woman,
her eyes bright but telling nothing.

"You could make her as strong as twelve
men," suggested the reindeer. "So that she can
defeat the Snow Queen."

The woman shook her head. "Twelve men
could not defeat the Snow Queen as well as this
little girl can, just as she is. Can't you see how
powerful she is? Crows talk to her; reindeer
carry her; even robbers help her. Her power is
in her goodness; nobody can defeat that."

She told the reindeer to take Gerda two miles

further north, to where the Snow Queen's
garden began, and to leave her there. "The rest
she will have to do herself."

"She will die!" said Ba sorrowfully.

But Gerda spoke up. "I must try," she said,
and climbed onto the reindeer's back once more.

The edge of the Snow Queen's garden was
marked with huge, jagged blocks of ice. Nothing
grew in it, but the snow fell so thickly there was
scarcely any air between the flakes.

Gerda slid to the ground and the reindeer
wept. She put her arms around his neck, "Dear
Ba," she said. "I hope we will see one another
again. But now I must hurry to save little Kay."

V

Gerda turned and ran into the freezing-cold snow. Very soon she could see nothing but snowflakes, which seemed to get larger and larger as she ran on. Then she realized that they were moving all by themselves, and closing in on her. They swirled into shapes of fearsome creatures — some looked like great, icy bears with razor-sharp teeth, and others were like huge, frosty serpents.

"Please spare me," Gerda breathed. Her breath came in white puffs into the cold air. Before her eyes, the little puffs of breath drew together, and became tall, white figures, with shields and spears. They surrounded her like guards and battled with the snowflake creatures. Gerda stumbled on, half frozen to death.

She reached the Snow Queen's palace, and slipped inside the jagged, frosty gates. The walls and floors of the palace were polished ice, and from the ceiling hung vast chandeliers, each made from hundreds of glittering icicles.

Gerda ran through the chilly corridors until she came to a cavernous hall. It was filled with a giant, frozen lake, shattered into countless pieces. In the middle of the lake was the Snow Queen's throne.

Luckily the throne was empty, as the Snow Queen was not at home. Before she left, she had given Kay a task to keep him occupied. "Arrange these shards of ice to spell out the word 'ETERNITY'," she had told him, "and you shall be your own master. You may have the whole world to roam in, and a new pair of skates."

Since then, Kay had been pushing the huge
ice shards around, trying to arrange them into
letters. But he could barely think, let alone work
out how to do it. When Gerda came into the
hall, he was sitting on a block of ice in despair.

Gerda gave a cry of joy when she saw him.
"I've found you!" she said, rushing over to him.

But Kay could barely hear her. He was so
frozen into the Snow Queen's power that
nothing else could move him. He stared at
Gerda blankly.

Gerda wrapped her arms around him and
burst into tears. "I've come across the world
to take you home, Kay," she sobbed. "I love
you more than anything."

Suddenly, a tiny light appeared in the little
boy's eyes. Gerda kissed him on the cheek,

and warmth seeped into his body. She kissed him again, and roses bloomed in his cheeks.

All at once, Kay remembered everything. He looked at Gerda and saw his best friend standing there. "How could I have forgotten you?" he whispered, his eyes filling with tears.

As the tears spilled down his face, the ice splinter that had been lodged in his eye was washed away. The warm love in his heart melted the splinter that had been stuck there, too. At last, Kay was back to his old self.

He put his arms around Gerda and squeezed her tightly. Gerda squeezed him even more tightly and they both burst out laughing. Their laughter rang out across the hall, making the icicles chime and the great shards of ice sing in harmony.

Then something very strange began to happen. All the shards of ice in the hall began to move. They arranged themselves slowly into shapes. "They're making letters," said Gerda.

"I can't believe it..." Kay whispered, as the shards of ice spelled out the word that would set him free: 'Eternity'.

"Gerda, I'm free!" said Kay.

"Then what are we waiting for?" Gerda said pulling him to his feet. "Come on, quickly. Let's go home!" The two friends ran out of the hall.

But then a voice stopped them in their tracks. "Who goes there, sneaking away like thieves in the night?" it hissed, reaching through the corridors like fingers of ice.

The children's hearts thumped with terror. And then the Snow Queen appeared. She stalked down the corridor towards them, tall and cold and furious.

"Get back into the hall," she snarled, and her glare looked as if it would shatter the children where they stood.

"I will not," Kay said bravely. "The ice shards spell out the word 'Eternity'. You can go and see for yourself. Your power cannot hold me here any longer."

The two children slipped past the Snow Queen and ran out of the palace doors. They passed the fallen shapes of snow creatures, half crumbled where they lay, and ran on through the open, sparkling snow.

Behind them, the defeated Snow Queen let out a wail like shattering ice. But there was nothing she could do to stop them.

It seemed like no time at all before they had reached the tiny hut where the old lady lived, and where the reindeer was waiting for Gerda.

They told their story with sparkling eyes and flushed cheeks, over bowls of warming soup. Then the two children climbed onto the reindeer's back and set off for home.

Ba flew like the wind, his hooves barely touching the ground. The snow gradually petered out and the forest began. They went on and on through the trees, until they reached a meadow and a winding stream.

"I think we can find our way from here," said Gerda, slipping down from the reindeer's back. "Ba, thank you for everything you've done for us. Now it's time for you to go back to your homeland and be happy."

"I'll never forget you," Ba replied softly, and bowed his head for one last embrace.

Gerda and Kay found a little boat bobbing on the banks of the river. They climbed aboard and rowed back home.

Grandmother was there to welcome them, overjoyed to see them safe and sound. "Now *you* must have a story or two to tell *me*," she said.

A lot of time had passed since they had been away, but summer had come again. When Gerda and Kay went up to their roof garden, they found that the roses were just coming into bloom.

This photograph of Hans Christian
Andersen was taken when he was 60.

ABOUT HANS CHRISTIAN ANDERSEN

Hans Christian Andersen was born in 1805 in Odense, a small town in Denmark. His father was a poor shoemaker and his mother was a washerwoman. In many ways, his life was rather like a fairy tale. He went from rags to riches, and drew on his experiences to tell the stories that made him famous.

As a boy, Andersen didn't have many friends, but liked playing with puppets, listening to the traditional folk tales his grandmother told him and singing. He was nicknamed 'the little nightingale' because he had such a sweet voice.

At 14, Andersen set off to seek his fortune in the capital city, Copenhagen. It was two days away by stagecoach, but he didn't have enough money for the fare to take him all the way, so he finished the last 10 miles of the journey on foot. He arrived in the city on September 6, 1819. It was a new beginning for him, and he celebrated the date every year for the rest of his life.

At first, he tried to make a living as an actor and singer, while writing plays in his free time.

He hoped his plays would make his name, but he'd had only a very basic education, and his spelling was so bad that no one would take them.

When Andersen was 17, a generous director spotted his potential and arranged for him to go back to school. Andersen was a lanky teenager in a class of 11-year-olds from rich families, and he didn't fit in at all. Later, he described this as the most miserable time of his life, and perhaps the experience is reflected in his story *The Ugly Duckling*.

By the time he completed his education, Andersen was determined to find success as a writer. He experimented with different styles of writing, and toured Germany and Italy in search of inspiration. But it wasn't until he thought back to the stories his grandmother had told him as a boy that he began to write the fairy tales that would make him world famous.

His first stories for children were published in 1835, including *The Tinderbox* and *The Princess and the Pea*. Everyone loved them, so Andersen wrote more... and more...

The fairy tales were translated into many languages, and Andersen visited different countries, meeting other writers, and fans of all ages. In Germany, he met the Brothers Grimm who were famous for collecting folk tales; in England, he met Charles Dickens who, like him, had risen to fame as a writer after a childhood of poverty. Back in Denmark, he was even invited to drink hot chocolate – an expensive luxury at the time – with the king and queen.

On April 2, 1875, Andersen celebrated his 70th birthday with a lavish banquet for 244 people at which each dish was named after one of his fairy tales. Four months later, he died in his sleep.

But his stories live on. They have been made into movies, plays and ballets, as well as inspiring all kinds of artists, composers and writers. Andersen's fans flock to Copenhagen to see the statue of the Little Mermaid that was put up near the shore in his memory.

Every year, all over the world, International Children's Book Day is celebrated on or around April 2, Hans Christian Andersen's birthday.

TIMELINE

1805 Hans Christian Andersen is born in Odense, Denmark, on April 2.

1819 He moves to Copenhagen, hoping to pursue an acting career and make his fortune.

1822 At 17, he starts at Slagelse Grammar School.

1829 His first book for adults is published and his first play is performed in Copenhagen.

1832 Andersen writes his first autobiography.

1835 The first two volumes of his *Fairy Tales for Children* are published. These include *The Princess and the Pea* and *The Tinderbox*.

1837 *The Little Mermaid* and *The Emperor's New Clothes* are among the stories published in his third volume of fairy tales.

1838 The King of Denmark awards Andersen an annual grant to support his work. A fourth volume of fairy tales is published, including *The Brave Tin Soldier*.

1843 More fairy tales are published, including *The Ugly Duckling* and *The Emperor and the Nightingale*, which was partly inspired by Jenny Lind, a Swedish opera singer who was nicknamed 'the Swedish nightingale'.

1844 *The Fir Tree* and *The Snow Queen* are published.

1845 Meets the brothers Grimm while visiting Berlin.

1846 A second autobiography, *The True Story of My Life,* is published.

1847 Visits England and meets Charles Dickens.

1855 A third autobiography, *The Fairy Tale of My Life,* is published.

1857 Returns to England and stays with Dickens.

1872 His final volume of stories is published and he begins to suffer from symptoms of liver cancer.

1874 Appointed a Privy Councillor for Copenhagen.

1875 Andersen dies on August 4.

USBORNE QUICKLINKS

For links to websites where you can find out more about the life and works of Hans Christian Andersen, go to the Usborne Quicklinks Website at www.usborne-quicklinks.com and type in the keywords 'Hans Christian Andersen'.

The recommended websites are regularly reviewed and updated but, please note, Usborne Publishing is not responsible for the content of any website other than their own. We recommend that children are supervised while using the internet.

Designed by Nancy Leschnikoff and Jessica Johnson
Managing Designer: Nicola Butler; Editorial Director: Jane Chisholm
Digital imaging by John Russell and Nick Wakeford
Cover designed by Helen Lee

Every effort has been made to trace the copyright holders of material in this book. If any rights have been omitted, the publishers offer to rectify this in any subsequent editions following notification. The publishers are grateful to the following individuals and organizations for permission to reproduce material on the following pages:
page 272, © Bettmann/CORBIS ; page 277, © Prisma Bildagentur AG / Alamy